ISLAMIC CLASSICS FOR YOUNG ADULTS

RUMI
STORIES FOR YOUNG ADULTS
FROM THE MATHNAWI

TRANSLATED AND ADAPTED FROM THE PERSIAN BY

MUHAMMAD NUR ABDUS SALAM

ILLUSTRATIONS BY
ROSE GHAJAR BAKHTIAR

ABC INTERNATIONAL GROUP, INC.

Library of Congress Cataloging-in-Publication Data
    A catalog for this book is available from the Library of Congress

Rumi, Jalal al-Din translated by Muhammad Nur Abdus Salam, Ph.D.
    1. Islam—Young Adults 2. Islamic Literature
    I. Jalal al-Din Rumi II. Muhammad Nur Abdus Salam, Ph.D. III. Rose Ghajar Bakhtiar IV. Title

    ISBN: 1-930637-04-7

Printed in the United States of America

Cover Design by Liaquat Ali

Published by
ABC International Group, Inc.

Distributed by
KAZI Publications, Inc.
3023 W. Belmont Avenue
Chicago IL 60618
Tel: 7732-267-7001; FAX: 773-267-7002
email: info@kazi.org/www.kazi.org

CONTENTS

A FEW WORDS ABOUT RUMI

The 13th Christian century, roughly equivalent to the 7th Islamic century, was a time of disaster and peril for the Islamic world. It was the century of the Mongol invasions. Riding across the steppes of Central Asia on their sturdy horses, inspired on their mission to conquer the world and destroy settled civilization by their leader Chenghiz Khan, the eastern frontiers of Islam bore the brunt of the first terrible attacks which would eventually reach the heart of Europe.

By the time of Rumi's birth the fabled cities of Samarqand and Bukhara were already in the hands of the pagan Kara-Khitay Turks. The Mongols were moving westward behind them. During his lifetime, in 1258 C.E., the Mongols would reach and destroy Baghdad. They would mercilessly slaughter its inhabitants and execute the last Abbasid caliph by wrapping him in a carpet and trampling him to death under the hooves of their horses. Central Asia, Iran, Afghanistan, eastern Turkey, Iraq, and most of Syria, that is, about half the Islamic world of the time, became part of the Mongol Empire.

Nor were the Mongols the only threat. In the far west Christian crusaders were retaking Spain. By the end of the century, only the kingdom of Granada was left in

Muslim hands. And in Palestine and along the coast of the eastern Mediterranean, other crusaders continued to linger in scattered strongholds even though their main strength had been broken by Salah al-din in the previous century.

Such a series of military and political disasters would not strike the Islamic world again until the period of European domination began with Napoleon's invasion of Egypt in 1798.

In such uncertain and dangerous times, when the world is confused and in chaos, people often turn to God for help and answers to problems and circumstances that seem beyond their control. Twelfth century Islam was no exception: it was a century of heightened spirituality and a general turning to Sufism and other mystic movements for inner peace and salvation in a world gone mad with warfare and the lust for power.

****

It was into this perilous world that a child named Jalal al-din was born on September 30, 1207, in the famous city of Balkh, now a sad ruin about twenty miles west of Mazar-i-Sharif in modern Afghanistan. His father was Baha 'l-din Walad, a writer, teacher, and a mystic in his own right. With the Mongols on the move in the direction of Balkh, Jalal al-din's father decided it was time to move away from the frontier.

About 1218 he left Balkh with his family and began to travel westwards, even as the Mongols were moving in the same direction. It is said that father and son met notable mystics and scholars on this journey, including Attar in Nishapur, and also performed the Pilgrimage to the Holy City of Makkah.

Eventually, the sultan of Konya invited Baha 'l-din and his family to settle in his city in 1228 CE. He became a religious teacher and the leader of the local Sufis. When he died in 1231, his son succeeded to the leadership of the Konya Muslims.

Now, Konya is in western Turkey. In those days, the memory of the Eastern Roman Empire was still fresh. Indeed, Constantinople was still the capital of the much-reduced empire. For this reason, Muslim classical writers, when they speak of Rum (Rome), are talking about Constantinople and the Eastern Roman Empire rather than the Rome we know in Italy. And since Konya was in the heart of this region, Jalal al-din came to be called Rumi, that is, the Roman. He is also called 'Mawlana,' a term of address reserved for respected teachers, so his full name with titles is often given thus: Mawlana Jalal al-din Rumi.

After becoming the leader of the Sufis, Rumi led the normal life of a teacher and spiritual leader. Had things continued thus, he would probably have remained a minor figure in the history of mysticism. A chance meeting with another spiritual guide in the fall of 1244 CE, changed his life and the history of mysticism forever. That man was Shams al-din of Tabriz. He was the spark that ignited the genius that lay dormant in Rumi's soul.

Rumi and Shams al-din became close confidants. Under his guidance, Rumi attained heights of spiritual ecstasy he had never dreamt of. Their association became so close that Rumi's disciples became jealous and tried to separate the two like-souls. In 1248 CE they succeeded and Shams al-din disappeared from history.

Rumi was devastated. He poured out his anguish in

one of the most remarkable volumes of all literature, the *Divan of Shams-i-Tabrizi* in which he, Rumi, became Shams al-din!

Later two other men, Salah al-din Zarkub and Husam al-din Chelebi, propelled Rumi forward on his mystic journey. Chelebi in particular seems to have been instrumental in encouraging Rumi to write his masterpiece, the *Mathnawi-yi-manawi* (the Spiritual Couplets). This colossal volume was apparently dictated by Rumi to Chelebi while the poet was in a state of ecstasy. It is one of the great literary treasures of the human mind searching for spiritual love and truth.

It is from the *Mathnawi* that the stories in this collection have been drawn.

Rumi's writings are not dead books of interest only to scholars. They are not exercises in artistic display. Instead, they possess the eloquence of simplicity. Even today, after more than seven centuries, his writings are readily accessible to Persian speakers, presenting fewer difficulties than Shakespeare does to the modern English speaker.

Rumi's writings may be enjoyed by Muslims and non-Muslims. They are of universal value because they deal with the eternal problems and dilemmas of life whether in the Middle Ages or today. Our outer circumstances may have changed over the centuries, but we face the same moral issues; we yearn for the same spiritual balance; and we ask the same questions about the meaning of life and death. Many have found guidance and hope in the inspired verses of Rumi. May you also.

Muhammad Nur Abdus Salam, Ph. D.

1

"THE DONKEY'S GONE! THE DONKEY'S GONE!"

O nce there was a poor Sufi. He had a donkey which he would ride on in his travels from one place to another. During the day he would travel about as was his custom and at night, if he should come upon a house of dervishes or an inn, he would spend the night in their company. If he did not find such a place, he would sleep in a mosque or in some ruins. He used to say to himself, "Wherever night falls, there is my bed."

Since the dervish had no family and owned nothing, and he possessed no skills, to live he would recite poetry about morals and in praise of the prophets and religious leaders in villages and towns and then move on. He was able to survive on the gifts of money, food, and other articles that the people gave him. In his own world he was content and he thanked God for His bounty.

The only thing the dervish owned other than the clothes on his back was that very donkey. With it he was able to roam God's world and learn lessons from the world's good and evil. He didn't spend much time thinking

11

about food and eating. He used to say, "An open mouth does not remain without its daily bread. As long as it is my portion and fate, there will be enough to keep me alive from whatever source. All that is needed is a heart free from the worry about what I have and don't have."

And this freedom, too, the dervish had.

One day when the dervish was crossing a desert with his donkey and he was tired, exhausted, hungry, and thirsty, he came upon a village. He drank water from the first irrigation ditch he came upon and washed his face and hands. While refreshing himself he gave his donkey to drink its fill, then he went in search of a dervish inn.

Some men pointed out a garden and said that there was such an inn there. So the dervish went to it and looked at the Sufis and dervishes that were gathered there. He led his donkey to the stable and after putting some hay into the manger, he told the stable hand to groom the animal. Then he went back to the assembly of dervishes.

There were many different kinds of dervishes at the inn. There were upright Sufis and tired dervishes; there were broken-hearted beggars and tight-lipped rogues; in short, all kinds of men.

The Sufis and dervishes welcomed the new arrival and greeted him warmly. But the rogues in the inn, who had seen the newcomer arrive with a donkey that he had put in the stable, made more of a fuss over him than any of the others and showed him much honor.

One of the rascals prayed loudly to God for the new-comer's good health in the manner of true dervishes. Another showed him to the place of honor in the assembly. Still another with great warmth asked him how he was and gently engaged the new arrival in conversation, while still others signaled and gestured to each other and then left the assembly quietly. In truth, they were always in wait for such an event: that a stranger would come to them and have something of value with him that they could use for themselves. And now this dervish had arrived with a donkey which was now tied up in the stable!

The scoundrels collected together and headed straight for the stable and stole the dervish's donkey. In another street they sold the animal to a passerby who was ignorant of what had happened. The thieves then spent the money on food and drink and sweetmeats and whatever else they fancied and returned to the inn.

Yes, they returned and gleefully invited all in the assembly to share in a feast in honor of their recently arrived guest. They all exclaimed, "The pleasure of the arrival of a dervish is love!"

The dervish was very pleased with the hospitality of the inn. They all ate a heavy supper of many kinds of food and enjoyed the sweets and various drinks, having a good time as dervishes will. The dervish was offered tidbits and made to feel welcome by all present. They shook the dust off his clothes and kissed his hands and prayed for his well-being. They beseeched the Lord for the his glory. The party grew more animated as the night wore on. Gradually the Sufis began to recite poetry and clap hands. Soon they were stamping and dancing.

At a signal from the thieves, the minstrel began to sing and beat a drum. Since he knew about the theft and the sale of the dervish's donkey, that was the first thing that occurred to him to sing about. So he beat his drum and sang this verse in a loud voice:

> "Joy has come and sorrow has gone;
> The donkey's gone, the donkey's gone,
>   the donkey's gone,
> The donkey's gone, the donkey's gone!"

The thieves joined in the minstrel's song and sang loudly:

> "The donkey's gone, the donkey's gone!"

Everyone was excited and shouting. They jumped up and down and continued to repeat that verse.

Now the visiting dervish, when he saw the liveliness of the men, forgot his own exhaustion. Thinking that the words "the donkey's gone!" had some special significance to the dervishes at the inn, he joined in the singing. He began to enjoy himself so much that he sang more loudly than the rest: "The donkey's gone! The donkey's gone!"

The party continued for a couple of hours and then, when the hour had become late and they were worn out from their singing and dancing, some of the dervishes left while another group stayed at the inn. Our dervish, too, stayed behind and since he was tired from his journey, he found a spot and went to sleep.

Early the next morning all of the dervishes left on their own business while our Sufi woke up later than the rest. After making ready to travel and not knowing what had happened, he went to the stable to take his donkey, but the animal was not in the stable!

He thought to himself, the groom has probably taken

the donkey for a drink of water, but when the groom came back he did not bring the dervish's donkey with him.

"Where's my donkey?" the dervish demanded of the groom.

"What donkey?" the groom sneered.

"What do you mean?" cried the dervish. "The donkey I put in your charge last night!"

The groom made fun of the dervish. "Look at his long beard!"

The dervish grew agitated. "My good fellow, what kind of talk is this? I'm telling you to bring my donkey and you're making fun of me? Are we bosom buddies to fool around together? Hurry up! Bring the donkey! I want to get started. If you think you can get rid of me with this nonsense you've got another thing coming! I'll go to the judge and lodge a complaint against you! I'll disgrace you!"

The groom snapped, "You're the one who is the fool, my good fellow! Where do you think all that food and drink, hot and cold, that we consumed last night came from? It all came from the money they got for selling the donkey. Right?"

"O my God!" wailed the dervish. "My donkey? Who gave you permission to sell my donkey?"

The groom replied, "I didn't sell it. The thieves sold it."

"Then why did you give them my donkey? Wasn't I its owner?"

"Well, they were too many for me. They were ten men and they scared me. They told me that were going to take the donkey and if I said anything they'd take revenge on me. I was afraid for my life so I stayed quiet. They even left two men with me to make sure that I didn't go the party. Yes, sir, that's the way it was, until the affair heated up and no one knew what he was doing."

"Supposing that what you say is true," said the dervish, "and they took the donkey in broad daylight, I was still here! You should have let me know a half hour, an hour, or a couple of hours later so that I could recognize them and start a fight with them. I could have gotten good men to arbitrate between us and try to get my money back. That wouldn't have put you in any danger."

The groom nodded. "That is true. In fact, two hours after the festivities had started I went there to call you and let you know what had happened, but when I went in, I saw that you were enjoying yourself and making more of a commotion than anyone else! You yourself were celebrating the donkey's departure, dancing, and bellowing 'The donkey's gone! The donkey's gone!'

"I figured that you knew about the affair and there was nothing more for me to say," continued the groom. "I said to myself that the dervish is an upright man, a saint, and he seems to delight in making the other dervishes happy by selling his own donkey and using the money for a party. If you were in my place, what would you have done?"

The dervish admitted that the groom was right. "Now I realize this was all my own mistake. I followed them in their behavior blindly without understanding or knowledge. I became as one of them. If I had thought about the meaning of 'the donkey's gone' from the very beginning, none of this would have happened. Now there is nothing I can do. It was my blind imitation of their behavior that caused you to misunderstand the situation. If I had not sung the song of the thieves more loudly than they did, I would not have lost my donkey."

Blindly copying others destroys a people,
Two hundred curses on such blind imitation!

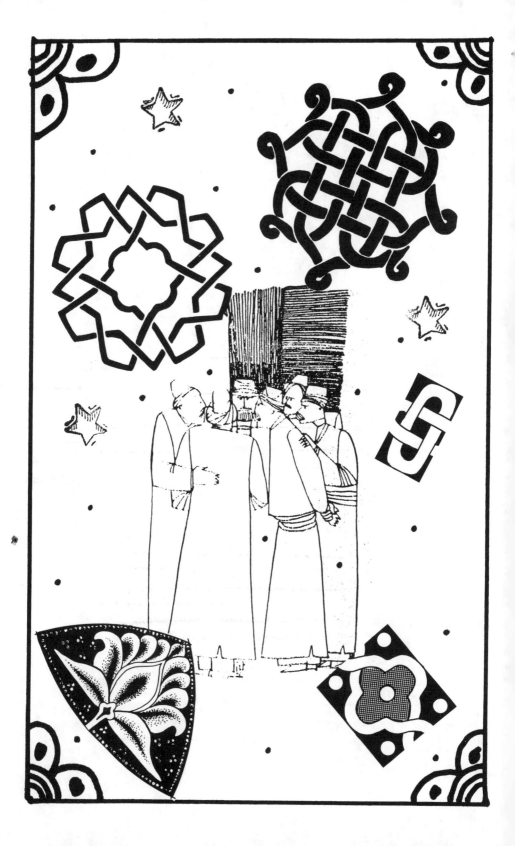

moral: stand up for what you think is right

2
SAVED BY THE BEARD!

Once there was a great king named Sultan Mahmud who liked to roam about at night. As we know, in ancient times the work of government departments was not as well-organized as it is today, so it frequently happened that rulers did not know much about the conditions of their subjects. Government officials, princes, and others who ran the country's affairs often oppressed the people, took bribes, and lied about matters.

And so it happened that for these reasons, some kings who wanted to be better informed about their people would go about the city at night disguised as dervishes, beggars, or nightworkers. They would be accompanied by one of their trusted confidants. Unknown to the public, they would go about the city and learn about the conditions. They would ask about the prices of goods. If they heard the sound of weeping or wailing, they would enquire from the servants about the cause. If they saw a group of men gathered together, they would join them to see what was happening. For the same reasons, they would enter the mosques, too. They would look in on ceremonies of mourning and celebrations in order to learn what the people were doing and saying. If they heard them complaining about the sheriff or other government officials, they would either remove the miscreants from their posts or punish them.

In short, the would get accurate and sound information firsthand from the people. This enabled them to better attend to the people's affairs, thereby making the rulers more beloved and respected by their subjects.

There are many stories about the adventures of Shah Abbas of Esfahan and other monarchs who wander about the city streets at night. However, this story is about Sultan Mahmud.

One evening Sultan Mahmud dressed himself as a laborer and went out to roam the streets of Ghaznin (in modern Afghanistan) by himself. It was a winter night and the streets were empty and the doors closed. Once in a while he saw a dog or a beggar or some other person moving about. The king decided to go to the edge of the city to see if the guards and police were doing their duties.

He came upon an open space and saw four or five men standing at one side whispering together. When the king tried to approach them, they blocked his way, saying, "Wait up there! Let's see who you are and where you're going."

Mahmud replied. "Nowhere. I'm just a man like yourselves wandering the streets as you are. The difference between us is that I'm not bothering you, but you are questioning me."

One of the four snapped, "Okay, we don't have time to fool around with you. How much money to you have in your pockets?"

Sultan Mahmud laughed. "Hah! If I had any money in

talent: shakes his beard he gets set free

my pockets, do you think I would be walking around like this? I'd be sleeping in my bed! I'm thinking about how to lay my hands on some money! But anyway, what business is it of yours?"

"This is marvelous!" they answered. "It seems that you are one of us! Since that is the case, if you are clever you can join up with us. We, too, are wondering where there is money to be found tonight. Do you have any ideas? We can't find work and we don't have any food. We are night rovers, and tonight we plan to steal something. Right now we are making our plans, but it's going to be a tough job. We have to climb over walls and open doors by any means possible. We must be quiet and ready to run away. The owner of the house may be awake! A policeman may come upon us! Our work is dangerous and can land us in prison. In short, you've got to have the aptitude. Do you think you've got it?"

Sultan Mahmud, who had never encountered such men before, had an inclination to go with them so that he could discover what they were up to.

So he answered, "I don't know. I've never done anything like that. But if you'll take me, I'll come along. If not, I'll go about my own business."

The thieves said, "No, no you don't! Now that you know us we can't let you go because you might squeal on us to a policeman or set a trap for us. We'll have to tie you up and hide you in some desolate ruins so that no one would be able to hear you. But if you want to come with us, you've got to know what to do to be of any use to us. We don't need a partner who doesn't know what he's doing."

"What a fix I'm in," Mahmud replied. "For example, what do I have to know how to do? You fellows don't have

forbid him

a workshop that needs a skilled worker! You just go over walls and take people's property. All right, I'll help."

The thieves laughed. "Not so fast! Each one of us has a skill useful in our work."

One of them said, "Mine is in my ears. When a dog barks I understand what he is saying. I can tell the difference between a bark meaning a thief is approaching and a bark meaning that the dog is hungry."

"Mine is in my eyes," said the second thief. "Whenever I see someone in the darkness, I can identify him in daylight no matter how he is dressed. This is important because when we want to sell the stolen goods we don't want to approach the wrong man and get in trouble."

Said the third," My value is in my arms. I can cut holes in walls and tear doors off their hinges so quietly that not a sound is heard."

"Mine is in my nose," said the fourth thief. "I sniff the earth and can tell where it's from. I can distinguish between the smell of a goldsmith's shop and that of a harness maker's."

"And mine is in my hands," said the fifth man. "When we have to throw a rope over a wall to climb over it, I throw the hook with such skill that it holds firm and we can climb over."

"So, if we take you along what can you do?" asked the thieves. "What skill do you possess that will be of use to us?"

Mahmud thought a little, then said. "All of your abilities are useful, but mine is far more important. Your skills are of use when you haven't been caught, but if you are caught by a policeman or a householder, none of your skills will help you. However, the art which I possess is very marvelous. It is in my beard. It grants freedom and salvation. If a criminal falls into the hands of a policeman or an executioner, I wiggle my beard by talking and he is set free immediately!" ✳ special talent

"O God!" cried the thieves. "Fantastic! Your skill is much more important than ours! What a wonderful beard you have! You are our leader, our pillar, our chief! We're ready to give you a greater share of the goods and because we can do our jobs free from worry. Let's go! Let's not waste any more time."

They turned right, into the lane and started off. When they had gone a little way, a dog fled from in front of them and barked.

The thief with the skillful ears declared that the dog said that an important man is accompanying you.

The others said, "Yes, he must mean our new friend whose beard can save us."

They came upon a low wall. One of them said that it would be very easy to climb over, but the man with the skillful nose sniffed about and said, "Don't bother. This is the wall of the house of a poor widow."

A short while later they came to a high wall above which trees could be seen. The man with the skillful hands threw the rope over the wall, made it firm. They climbed over the wall and found themselves in a garden. When they reached a building, the man with the skillful nose sniffed the earth.

"We've found a good place. I can smell a treasure of jewels."

Then, in a safe dark spot, the man with the skillful arms dug into the earth and found the treasure under a wall. He took out as much as he could of gold, silver, jewels, and other valuable articles and then they escaped to some ruins near the city moat and buried it all. As dawn was near, they said, "Now we shall separate. Tomorrow night, we'll come back to divide the loot."

So it was agreed that one of them, disguised as a beggar, would hang around the ruins until the next night as a guard. Before separating they said to Mahmud, "So far, so good. You come tomorrow night, too, and get your share."

disguise

Sultan Mahmud left them and returned to his palace, but not before he had memorized the place and their plans.

The next morning he told the responsible vizier what had happened and sent several officers and soldiers to seize the treasure and capture the thieves and bring them bound and chained to the Hall of Justice.

Thus the terrified thieves stood trembling in the line of criminals at the royal palace. When their turn came, the judge recited their crimes to them and said, "The people are tired of the activities of you night thieves. As an example to others, I order that these men be punished! Summon the executioner!"

The executioner had not yet had time to arrive when Sultan Mahmud, dressed in his robes of state, entered the hall and took his place on the throne. At this juncture, the man with the skillful eyes, the one who could recognize anyone he had seen at night by day, motioned to his comrades and said, "Look! The man who has the skillful beard and was with us last night is that very Sultan Mahmud!"

The thief with the skillful ears confirmed what the first had said. "Indeed, the dog that barked at us last night said that a great man was with us. He meant the king!"

At that moment the executioner entered the assembly

and the judge asked the thieves, "Do you confess to your crimes?"

The thieves answered, "Yes, we confess, but if you want to do justice, you must punish us all together. Last night we were six men together who stole the treasure. We are but five."

"Show us the sixth man," ordered the judge.

"Be patient," they said. Each one of us had a special ability, and each of us demonstrated that ability. Now we are awaiting another to demonstrate his ability. There is someone who can set us free."

"In any case," said the judge, "I have to order the executioner to punish you. No one except the king can grant you pardons."

A smile played on Sultan Mahmud's lips while all stood waiting. The thieves did not have the audacity to reveal the secret that they knew. Then one of the five recited this verse in a loud voice:

"We all have all used our skills;
O great one, now wiggle your beard!"

And Sultan Mahmud broke into laughter at this verse and commanded that since this was the first time they had done this and the loot had been recovered, they should be pardoned. Each one of them repented their crimes.

After that, the king commanded that each one be given a job in keeping with his skill.

Then he addressed them, saying, "I have promised pardons and I have delivered pardons. But after this, for every crime there shall be a punishment!"

3
ESCAPE FROM DEATH

It is said that one day a little before noon, when the prophet Solomon was sitting in his audience chamber in Jerusalem, a flustered man rushed in. It was plain from his appearance that he was terrified and frightened.

"What's wrong? What do you want?" Solomon asked him.

"O great one!" the man began. "I have just seen Azrail, the Angel of Death, today! He looked at me angrily, but passed me by. I'm afraid that he will come back and take my life."

"Calm down, calm down!" Solomon said. "Azrail is one of the angels and he brings life and takes it back only at the command of God. He won't do anything until he receives His order. I could see Azrail every day, but I would not be afraid. But, just because you are afraid, what can I do and what do you want from me?"

"But," the man replied," I have always been afraid of Azrail. Today, when I saw his angry look, I grew even more afraid. People say that the wind obeys Solomon. You can order the wind to take me to another land. People say that Solomon helps the needy. What I need now is that you immediately command the wind to carry me to India. Now that Azrail has seen me in this country I don't want to stay here a moment longer. This is my need and this is my request. Help me to escape Azrail and death!"

"Very well," Solomon declared. "Life and death are not in my hands, but the winds are. I shall fulfill your request. Lo! I command the wind to take you wherever you want to go!"

Solomon ordered the wind to come before him and addressed it thus: "Ask where this man wants to go and take him there!"

So the wind placed the man on the flying carpet of Solomon. Crossing deserts and rivers, the wind carried him far away to one of the cities of India within a few minutes. The man dismounted from the carpet and went about his own affairs.

That day passed. On the next day, Solomon met Azrail in the palace and spoke with him, "Azrail, a man came to me yesterday complaining about you. He asked me to order the wind to take him immediately to India to get as far away as he could from this city. I didn't want to disappoint him, so I did as he asked and sent him to India. But I wonder, why did you frighten him so much that you caused him to abandon his home and his business?"

Azrail replied, "I never do anything without the express command of God. I did not look at that man with anger. Yesterday I saw him in Jerusalem, and my look at him was one of astonishment, because I had received the command from God to take the soul of that very man in India! I was saying to myself, even if he could fly like a bird, he would never be able to reach India by the afternoon. Since his hour of death had not yet come, I looked at him with astonishment and passed him by. But later, at the proper time, I went to India and saw him there! Death took him there and I seized his soul."

Solomon nodded, saying, "That is so. You can escape from everything, but death is certain and cannot be escaped. It was his destiny to be in India at that hour. Since there was no means to carry him there except the wind, he himself came to me on his own feet and with his own tongue begged me and pleaded with me to send him there. And so he went to meet his destiny."

summary

- death is natural part of life & you can't escape it

- he was afraid of the angel

- you can try to escape death but you can't because it will find you

4
A LION WITHOUT A
MANE OR TAIL

Once there was an illiterate man who went one day
to a tattooer and said that he wanted to have a tattoo put on his arm.

In days of old, it was the custom for vagabonds, rogues,
and thugs to have tattoos tattooed on their arms, chests
and stomachs. The design of a lion or a leopard stood for
bravery. The picture of a friend or a loved one on their bodies was a sign of devotion to them, while a knife or a sword
meant strength and aggressiveness. In this way, they
could have their favorite picture with them at all times.

Most of the workers in the public baths knew how to
tattoo in addition to their other jobs. They shaved and cut
hair; they pulled teeth and circumcised children besides
tattooing. The tattooing was done in this way: First, the
skin was washed with boiled water. Then the picture of an
animal or some other thing was drawn on the customer's
body. After that, they scratched the skin with a needle following the lines of the design and rubbed various plant
dyes into the scratches. When the pain had gone away and

the wounds had healed the tattoo would remain on the body for the rest of the customer's life and not fade away.

Now this was unbecoming custom was disapproved of and educated people would never have tattoos put on their bodies, but in those days it was the custom of ignorant hoodlums.

So, the illiterate man went to the bath attendant who did the tattooing and said, "I want to be tattooed."

"Very good," the bath attendant replied. "What kind do you want?"

"I'm an athlete, strong and brave, and I want to have the tattoo of a lion on my body."

"Very auspicious!" exclaimed the attendant. "On what part of your body do you want the lion's picture?"

"On my right arm, near my shoulder."

"Very good,' said the tattooer. "Roll up your sleeve and sit down over there."

The customer sat down and the tattooer began his work. He washed the man's arm and plunged the needle into boiling water. He prepared some dyes and got some clean cotton. He brought the pen and inkpot and drew the picture of the lion on the man's arm. Then he set to work.

At the first prick of the tattooer's needle in his arm, the brave athlete felt a sharp pain and cried out, "Oh, my arm! What are you doing?"

"I'm doing what you asked me to do! Didn't you say you wanted the tattoo of a lion?"

"Of course," the strong man answered, "but from what point are you starting?"

"I started with the tail," the attendant replied. "Right at the tip of the lion's tail."

The man, whose arm was smarting from the prick of the needle, said, "All right, right now let's forget the tail and do the head and body. My lion won't have a tail. Let's suppose my lion's tail was cut off."

"No problem," said the tattooer. "We'll forget about the tail."

Then he started to work on the lion's head and decided to begin with the mane and neck. As soon as the customer felt the prick of the needle in his arm, he cried out again.

"Ouch! That hurts a lot. What are you doing?"

The tattooer said, "I'm making a lion. Relax a little and I'll be through in a little while."

The powerfully built athlete asked, "What part of the lion are you working on now?"

"The mane."

"Oh, my! The mane and the neck aren't important. What if my lion doesn't have a mane? The body will be enough."

"As you wish," said the bath attendant. "We'll forget about the mane, too."

Then the tattoo artist thought to himself, "Well, I can't start from the tail and I can 't start from the head. Why don't I start from the feet?" And he jabbed the point of the needle into the lion's paw drawn on the customer's arm.

Our hero yelled and howled. "What kind of a fussy and meticulous worker are you? The paws can't be seen. I don't want an art gallery on my arm. All I want is the shape of a lion. Forget the paws. My lion doesn't have any feet. Now do something so it doesn't hurt so much and hurry up and finish!"

"Yes, sir," said the bath attendant. "From now on I'll

just deal with the actual shape of the lion and forget about the details."

Then he looked at the picture of a lion he had drawn and decided to tackle the stomach. He brought the needle close to the man's arm.

Once again the strong man cried out and said, "Ouch! You're killing me with that needle! What are you doing? What part of the lion are you working on?"

"The most important part of the body of the lion, the stomach. There's no way to avoid it."

"No sir," said the athlete. "My lion doesn't need a stomach. Do something so that there is a lion, but with no stomach!"

The bath attendant was bewildered. He pondered the problem for a few minutes and then threw the needle into a corner of the room.

"Forgive me, mister champion," he said. "I'm very sorry. Until now, I've tattooed a thousand men and have drawn the picture of a lion on a man's body a hundred times, but I have never seen a lion without a mane or a tail or a stomach!

Who has ever seen a lion without a mane or a tail or a belly?

When did God ever create such a lion?

Since you can't put up with the pricks of the needle, it's better if you let your arm stay the way it is. Save me the bother, and stop pretending that you are a brave man and a lion-killer!

Since you cannot endure the prick of the needle,
Talk not of lions and fierce beasts!"

moral:- looks aren't
everything
- looks can be
deceiving

people's purposes & actions are
different

5
THE GROCER AND THE PARROT

Once there was a grocer who had a parrot. This parrot was not only very beautiful with a pleasant voice, but also was very intelligent. As the bird had spent a lot of time in the grocer's shop, he had come to know his owner's customers and would greet them and ask how they were.

When the grocer had to go out on some business, he would sometimes put the parrot, who had strings tied to his legs, on the counter. Then the grocer would go home for a while. The parrot knew that when his master was out of the shop, no one had the right to take anything from the shop, so he would say to anyone who came in, "Hello! Please be patient! The grocer will return shortly."

The people who knew about this were used to it, but when a stranger entered the shop saw the parrot behaving as though he were on guard, the person would be astonished and either wait until grocer returned, or leave and come back later.

Things went smoothly in this fashion, until one day a strange cat entered the shop because it had heard the

37

sound of a mouse. When the cat pounced on the mouse, the parrot got frightened for he had never seen such a thing! In order to save his life, he flew off the counter to take refuge in a corner of the shop, but the string tied to his legs caught on a large bottle of peanut oil. The bottle fell to the floor and shattered. The oil spilled out. The parrot flew up to his cage and sat on top of it, while the cat, scared by the sound of feathers and beating wings, scurried out of the shop.

When the grocer returned from his house, at first he didn't notice anything unusual and went to his customary place. Then he looked around and saw the broken bottle of oil. He looked at the bird and saw that its talons and feathers were splashed with oil and realized that the parrot had knocked the bottle down.

The grocer was upset about this and grabbed the parrot. He swore at him and used bad language. Then he said, "Ugly bird with a disagreeable voice! Now you have the impudence to break a bottle of oil. Take this!"

He snatched up a piece of wood that was lying nearby and cracked the parrot on the head with it and then threw the bird into a corner of the shop.

The blow had cracked the parrots head and torn its skin. A little while later the grocer was sorry for what he had done and tried to make up with the bird; however, the parrot who had been cursed and beaten would not utter a single word.

The grocer dressed the wound on the parrot's head, but after it had healed, there was a scar, a bald spot without feathers. The parrot still remained silent and would not speak. No matter how much the grocer or his customers

coming and going tried to get the bird to speak, it was of no use.

The grocer had always enjoyed listening to the bird's entertaining chatter and considered the bird the glory of his shop. Now he deeply regretted having struck the parrot, but the stubborn bird refused to break his silence.

The grocer's friends and acquaintances asked about the bird and the reason for its silence. They asked about the scar on the bird's head, too. The grocer would reply:

"I came back and found that the parrot had broken a bottle of oil. I got angry and hit him on the crown of his head with a stick. Now his head is bald and his tongue silent."

After a while the parrot, hearing the grocer repeatedly tell the customers the story of his breaking the bottle and spilling the oil and the explanation of his bald head, comprehended that he was bald because he had broken the bottle, spilled the oil, and had been beaten by the grocer.

So he went to a mirror, sat in front of it and studied the reflection of his bald head.

"Yes," he said. "The bottle broke and. . . and. . . and. . ." And he said no more.

In order to get the parrot to talk again, the grocer talked a lot more with customers. He told them stories about the parrot's voice and how he used to speak. But no matter how much he showed his fondness for the bird, it was no use. The parrot knew that he had broken the bottle, spilled the oil, been beaten, and had become bald. It was better to keep quiet.

Things remained this way until one day a number of acquaintances and neighbors of the grocer happened to be gathered in the shop, talking about many different things.

One of the men was bald, and had no hair on his head. After he had gone, one of the others remarked, "I know him. Up until a few years ago he had thick curly locks and a forelock, but now—I don't know why—he has lost his hair and is as bald as a bowl."

At that moment the parrot suddenly found his voice. "I know the reason! He broke the bottle and spilled the oil! He was beaten for that and he became bald!"

Upon hearing these words, everyone present broke into laughter, because they realized that the bird had been so preoccupied by his own bald head, that he had compared it with the head of a man!

The grocer was delighted to hear his parrot speak at last and said, "The words of the parrot are a good lesson for all of us. Sometimes in our deeds, we measure things by our own selves. For example, someone does something bad and gets caught. Afterwards he thinks that everyone in trouble is guilty. Or, the other way, an innocent person gets in trouble and thinks that everyone in trouble is innocent. But in truth one person's actions cannot be compared with those of another.

6

THE SIMPLE-MINDED CAMEL DRIVER

O nce there was a man who was a carouser, and a pleasure-seeking glutton. He wanted everything, but he had no special talent. In addition, he was very lazy and knew nothing of hard work. After he had squandered the property he had inherited from his father, he existed for a while by borrowing and not repaying. He would buy on credit and sell for cash. In short, he lived by cheating and fraud.

Several times he bought goods from a merchant on credit, promising to pay within six months. He would then sell the goods for half their value and spend the money. He often rented a house and bought furnishings on time, then moved away without giving notice to open his shop in another place. He sold goods entrusted to him as security and afterwards fled. In this way he was able to live for a time by defrauding other people of their goods.

However, since the out-of-balance load never reaches its destination and dishonesty always brings shame, one day one of his creditors caught up with him. When his sordid record became public knowledge, no one else would give him any more time to pay, or rest from demands for repayment. The penniless fraud was thrown in prison where he languished for some time.

Now, as a man without any money in a place had no respect or credit, he grew to like the prison and said to himself, "If I don't have anything else, here the prison puts clothes on my body and food in my stomach."

So he stayed in prison and since he didn't know any place worse than a prison that he could be sent to, he started to steal things belonging to others. He ate one man's lunch and another man's dinner. Wherever he saw a morsel, he wouldn't rest until he had gotten hold of it. He cast justice aside and forgot about mercy. He thought of nothing except filling his own stomach. Naturally, the other prisoners suffered from his actions and complained to the warden. The judge was informed and he went to inspect the prison personally.

The prisoners protested to the judge, "Isn't the misery of being prisoners enough for us that this vile man has also become an affliction upon us? He eats everything he sees. No one in the prison is safe from him. We beg you to separate him from us or give us relief from his evil behavior in some other way."

The judge pondered the problem and then said, "You are right. A bare, dismal prison is supposed to make a person dislike it. But when a person enjoys prison, prison will not improve him and he gets to like the free food. I must expel him from prison and make him work. If he doesn't learn from that, then I'll have to sentence him to hard labor some place."

So the judge summoned the penniless man and told him that he must give written promises to repay his creditors and leave the prison.

"I don't have any money," protested the man. "I have nothing in this world, and the penniless person is under the protection of God."

"If don't have any money," said the judge, "no one can do anything to you, but a just witness must testify to your bankruptcy."

Said the man, "These prisoners can testify to that! I don't have any other witnesses."

"The prisoners are themselves criminals,'" answered the judge. "That is why they are in prison. Their testimony cannot be accepted. Furthermore, they have lodged complaints against you."

"Anyway," retorted the man, "I don't have anything. The best place for me is right here in prison!"

"A prison is for punishment," insisted the judge. "As you like prison life, you won't be punished by staying in prison! I shall send you out of prison. Since you are not ashamed of being a bankrupt, I shall have you paraded around the city and so that everyone may be notified not to sell you anything on credit. After that, it'll be up to you. Either you'll find work and earn your own bread, or, should you give trouble to people again, I'll either send you to a place of hard labor, or sentence you to death!"

The judge ordered that the man be taken to the city square and a donkey, a cow, or a camel be found for him to ride on. He was to be paraded through the city streets for a whole day until nightfall while a town crier pointed him out and told the people to remember him, saying, "This man lives on other people and claims that he is without money. From this day on, anyone who sells him anything on credit or lends him anything has no right to complain

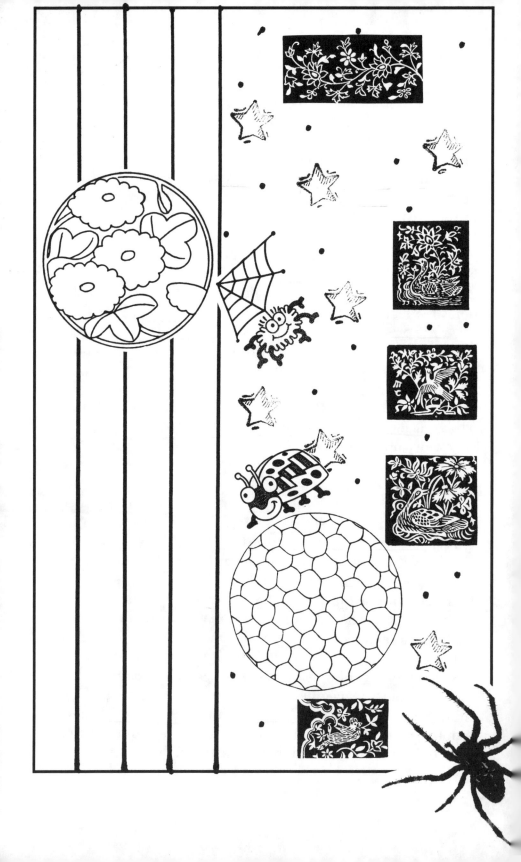

about him to the judge. Why? Because he is penniless and furthermore does not even fear prison!"

They thought that in this way he would be humiliated in the city and wouldn't be able to cheat anyone else. As a result, he would either have to get a job and work or leave the city.

So they took him to the city square where a crowd had gathered. A deputy of the judge spoke:

"Let's put this man on a donkey, a bull, or a camel and parade him through the city streets until nightfall. We shall explain to the people that he has no money or any other property."

At this moment a street vendor who sold firewood and had brought his load of firewood on a camel to sell to the townsfolk unloaded his animal and brought it to the crowd.

"Here is my camel. Put him on this!"

The judge's deputy said, "No, go about your business. We want an animal which is not being used for anything."

But the simple-hearted camel driver would not be put off. "My camel is better than any other animal," he said. Then he gave a small bribe to the judge's deputy; the deputy chose his camel.

So they placed the vagrant on the camel and led him around the city while a town crier shouted, "O people, look well at this man! He is a vagabond and doesn't have anything. He has cheated many people of a lot of money and goods, but his bankruptcy has been established before the judge. No one who sells anything to him on time or lends him money has a right to complain to the judge when this bankrupt doesn't pay it back. Mark him well and make sure you can recognize him in the future."

They stopped the camel at the head of every street and in every quarter to inform the onlookers about the man in the Persian, Luri, and Turkish languages. The simple-hearted camel driver was with them during all of this.

When night came, the bankrupt man was brought back to the main square of the city and taken off the camel. He was set free and the camel was returned to the camel driver and the officials dispersed. However, there were still a lot of people gathered around the poor man. When he wanted to leave, the camel driver took hold of his sleeve and said, "It's late and I have a long way to go. I have lost a lot of business today and haven't sold any firewood. You have been riding my camel from morning to night and I don't ask you to give me my expenses or pay me the fare. Just buy some fodder for the camel so that he doesn't go hungry."

"Take a look at this man!" cried the bankrupt. "What have we been doing from morning till night? What were they saying? Don't you have ears? Don't you have eyes? Don't you have a brain? The news of my shame and bankruptcy and poverty and helplessness has been shouted to the heavens and everyone has heard that I don't have a penny. Haven't you understood anything?"

"I don't know anything about such things," answered the camel driver calmly. "I only know that you have been riding my camel from morning till night. Give me what you owe me. If you don't I'll disgrace you!"

"You are really worse off than I am!" said the penniless man. "You're greedier than my creditors. All those to whom I owe money were trapped by their own greed, because they saw that I was buying goods on time at twice the going rate. I was spending more than my income, but they gave me their goods anyway out of greed for more profit. But you, you have heard from morning till night a thousand times that I don't have a penny! Haven't you understood yet? My good man, if I had any money and was about to pay people back, would I be taken through the city and disgraced like this? Now, if you have anything to say, tell it to the judge!"

*story about a bankrupt man who was better off in prison

· be content w/ what you have

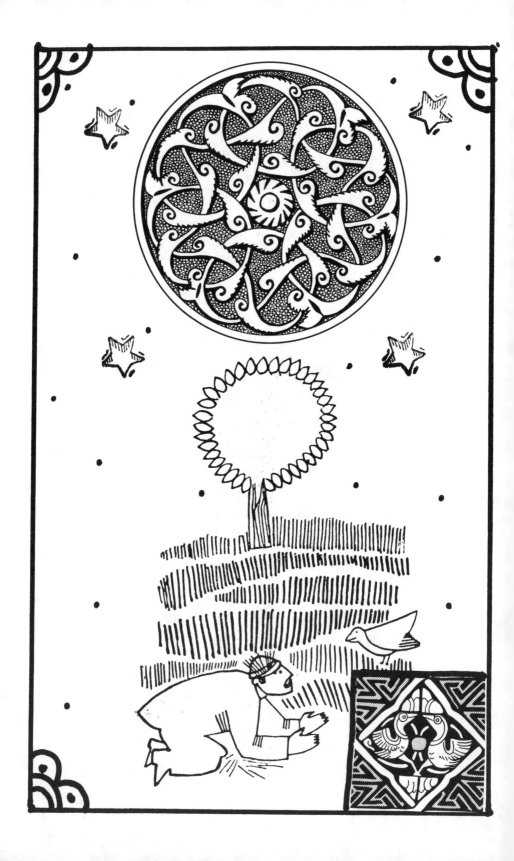

7
THE BAIT AND THE TRAP

One day a hunter went into the wilderness to hunt birds. He wandered about and came upon a meadow where from a distance he could see birds flying about. He prepared his bird snare and tied the top to the trunk of a tree. Then he scattered grains of wheat and millet under the snare. Taking the drawstring in his hand, he went a little distance away and sat beside a rosebush. He took some grass and greens and strewed them on his head and body. Then he remained motionless waiting to capture some birds.

Soon a swift bird, attracted from a distant region by the sight of the verdure, reached the spot and dropped down from the sky to land on a spot not far from the hunter. The bird began to search for seeds and grain.

As the bird drew nearer, the hunter sneezed. The bird understood from that sound that some person was near at hand. It looked about carefully. As soon as its eyes fell on the hunter covered with grass, it spotted him for what he was. So, it went away a little then sat in front of the hunter and asked him, "Who are you, grass-wearer, and what are you doing under the grass?"

"Dear bird," replied the hunter, "don't bother me and mind your own business. I am a pious, devout, and upright man and I am not interested in worldly things. I have left the world and its people. I am humbling myself here. I am spending my time worshipping God."

"That's something I haven't heard before," said the bird. "What does hiding under the grass in the middle of the wilderness to worship God mean? In my opinion, becoming a hermit and punishing oneself is not good. In order to worship God, it is not necessary to get under the grass and sit in a field. You can worship God in a city or a village, or wherever you live. There you could be of use to other people. Have you come here in idleness to worship God under the grass? Haven't you heard:

Worship is nothing but serving mankind;
It is not in rosaries, prayer rugs, and coarse robes."

"It is plain that you're an uneducated bird and don't understand people," said the hunter. "People are very evil and don't let each other rest in peace. They lie, they cheat. They trick and oppress each other. All they think about is the life of this world and worldly goods.

"As for myself," the hunter went on, "I am very sensitive and I can't stand to see such things. I, too, have worked a lifetime and tried to do good to people. Now that I have grown old, I want to be by myself and think about the next life. The plants of the field are food enough for me. The leaves of the trees are sufficient clothing. How long can one think just of this world?"

"What you say is true," replied the bird, "but you really aren't a wild animal of the open spaces. As long as he lives, a man must live with other men. If others are bad, you must be good. The bad will learn goodness from you. Think about it. If goodness is being the way you are now and everyone would like to run away from the world as you are doing, the affairs of the world will be crippled. A good deed is always that which can universally be done. What you are doing is not good and it isn't worship. Worship is something anyone can do and should make the world better instead of bringing about its ruin.

"All of the prophets, leaders, wise men, and good people," continued the bird, "have lived among the people and felt the troubles that other folk feel. Have you ever heard that a good person went to countryside and sat under grass to think only about himself? I have never heard of such a thing! It is selfish to forget about everyone else and think only about your own salvation."

"Leave me alone, bird," cried the hunter. "People have caused me a lot of trouble. Now, my neighbor's death was a lesson for me, and I can't forget death any more. It is really strange that now that I have run away from other people, you won't let me think about God. Please stop annoying me and mind your own business!"

"All right," said the bird and it started to go away. But after it had gone a few steps its eye fell upon the wheat and millet that was under the net. It thought to itself, "That's odd. I couldn't find any grain in the field, so why is there such a heap of it here?"

The bird really wanted to go and eat it, but it remembered the hunter's words: God, the Hereafter, worship, death. He was afraid that the grass-wearer might object, so it returned to the hunter and asked him, "Look here, is that wheat and millet yours?"

"No, my dear," the hunter answered. "It's not mine. I don't have a single piece of property, so how would I have wheat and millet? As far as I know, it belongs to two little orphans who have to come and take it away. Whatever you do, don't touch it! You can find other birdseed in the grass, so that is not lawful for you. Only someone who is deserving and dying of hunger can eat it. Anyway, it has nothing to do with me."

The bird whose mouth was watering for the food, couldn't pass the wheat up.

"As it happens," it said, "I'm deserving and dying of hunger. Suppose that someone like me is hungry. In such a case, even carrion flesh is lawful."

"I don't know," said the hunter. "I have nothing to do with such things. You know your own situation better than I do. Anyhow, if you are not deserving, then it is a sin to eat it. If you are, no one will stop you."

"If that's the way it is," said the bird after some thought, "I'll just eat a few grains. That will be enough to keep me alive. No matter who owns it, there is nothing wrong with that!"

Saying this, the bird went forward and began to eat. But it was caught in the snare with its first bite and quickly understood that it could not escape from the net. Then it realized that all of the hunter's talk of prayer and worship was meant to deceive him. The hunter had gained his objective, so he came out from under the grass to take the bird.

Said the bird, "I know what I've done. This befits a person who is tricked by a pious liar, a fake worshipper, and world-abandoning trickster."

"I don't know the person you are talking about," said

the hunter, "but there is no one here but the two of us. I was not talking nonsense to deceive you. I said that I was humbling myself and you said that you were deserving of the food. Tit for tat, one lie cancels the other.

"So, now you eat the wheat and I'll eat you. That way I'll get the reward for my humility and worship. But you must agree that it was your own greed that tricked you. People fall into traps because of their own greed. If I hadn't sneezed, you wouldn't have seen me and would gone straight to eat the wheat and fallen into the snare. You should have thought that wherever there is a bait there is a trap. You did it yourself, and there is no way to escape the results of your own actions."

8
THE GARDENER'S STRATEGY

One day three friends who had similar ideas and tastes were walking. They said, "Let's go to a village for a few days and stroll around its meadows and gardens. We'll enjoy ourselves."

One of them was a Sufi wearing the cap of a dervish, another was wearing a turban wound in the fashion of a mullah, while the third was a gentleman wearing a green shawl in the fashion of the sayyids, or descendants of the Prophet. These three were not used to doing any work, but they were used to sponging off the good people of whatever place they went to.

So they went out of the city together and entered a village. They viewed every place and promptly made a beeline for one of the gardens, the door of which happened to be open. Entering and seeing that there was no one in the garden, they settled beneath a tree. Each of the three went off to pick some fruit and then they sat together in the shade of that tree to eat and converse and joke together.

Just before noon, the gardener returned from the fields and went into the garden carrying a shovel on his shoulder. He saw his three uninvited guests sitting comfortably in the middle of the garden eating his fruit.

Now the gardener had watered the garden in the cold of winter and toiled in it day and night in the hope of a good harvest of fruit, so when he saw their calm indifference, he became very upset. He wanted to confront them, bawl them out, and kick them out of his garden.

But before he showed himself to them, he paused to reflect. If they were responsible types, they wouldn't enter a man's garden and eat its fruit without permission. Wearing such fine dress they wouldn't lay themselves open to the reproaches of others. From their actions and behavior it was obvious that they were worthless spongers and nothing he could say would affect them.

Therefore, he said to himself, "I am but one person and they are three thoughtless ruffians. If I object to their behavior, things may pass from words to blows, and there is no way I can take on the three of them. So, it's best that I first make a plan and adopt a strategy that will make them fall out with each other. Then I can handle them one by one."

The gardener made up his mind and laid down his shovel. He picked a bunch of grapes from a vine and approached them with a smiling face.

"Welcome! Welcome! How are you?"

They replied to his greeting. Since they knew they had done wrong, they were surprised at the warmth of the gardener's greeting and didn't know what else to say. The gardener went closer and sat on the ground near them and began to talk.

"Yes sir, this is incredible! I was lonely today and bored and God sent you here to be my company so that we could talk together. Well, how are you?"

They said, "Praise be to God, not bad. We too wanted to see you. We felt it in our hearts."

"Again you are very welcome!" the gardener said enthusiastically. "But this won't do. You didn't bring any rugs or blankets to make yourselves comfortable. We have a high regard for guests here."

While he was chatting in this way, he was looking them over carefully and saw that the Sufi dervish was the most worthless of the lot. So he turned to him and said, "Friend, I'm very tired, but there's a big carpet (gilim) in that room at the side of the garden. If it's not too much trouble, please bring it over here so that you can spread it and sit comfortably upon it. Then I'll think about lunch."

The Sufi got up and went to bring the carpet. While the Sufi was away, the gardener bent his head to the sayyid and the mullah.

"Brothers, I have taken a liking to the two of you because one of you is a learned mullah who frequents mosques and prayer niches, and the other is a descendant of the Holy Prophet and a crown on our heads. I am your servant.

"But I don't understand," he went on, "why you two worthies have brought that idle, lazy, freeloading Sufi dervish with you. He has no claim on me. If he were not with you, you two could stay here a week or however much you wanted to. I would be your host. But on the condition that I throw that lazy good-for-nothing out of the garden. Then we can all enjoy ourselves."

The gardener's tempting proposal impressed the men. They decided that it wasn't a bad idea at all.

"You're right, mister," they said. "We haven't been happy with that dervish either. He forced us to let him accompany us. So, when he returns, you can do with him as you like. He's nothing to us."

"Very good," said the gardener. "I'll take care of him right now."

Then they sat silently until the dervish returned with the carpet. Then the gardener said to him. "Look here, dervish! I've known this sayyid and this mullah for a long time and I am happy to have them as my guests. But to tell the truth, I don't care much for Sufis and dervishes. You'd better think about going elsewhere. Take a few apples and go away in peace. Go somewhere else. God will give you your food in another place."

Seeing that things were going against him, the dervish looked at his friends and saw them lowering their eyes to avoid his. They remained silent and made no move to support him. There was nothing for him to do but nod his head and say to his companions, "Very well. I'll go. It's obvious that you have come to some agreement among yourselves. But, the way I see things, you'll get little good from this garden and that gardener out of this betrayal of friendship."

The mullah and the sayyid replied, "This isn't any of your business anymore!"

The dervish turned away and left the garden.

Seeing that his plan had worked very well indeed, the gardener jumped up, grabbed his stick, and ran after the dervish. Catching him at the wall of the garden, he snarled at him, "You lowlife! Have you no shame? You enter a man's garden without permission and eat his fruit without paying? Which teacher or spiritual guide ordered you to freeload off of the people? Get away from here as fast as you can! If you don't, I'll summon the villagers and we'll teach you a lesson that you won't forget as long as you live!"

Then the gardener used his stick on the man until the dervish fled as fast as he could.

After the gardener had finished his work with the dervish, he returned and said the two remaining, "God willing, you'll forgive me. I didn't want to beat him at first, but when he started to talk back and use bad language, I decided to teach him a lesson. Anyway, now we three can enjoy ourselves."

He sat down with them and lit a pipe and began to smoke it while he thought, "There are still two of them and I can't take them both on by myself."

He resumed his conversation, saying, "It's nearly noon and it's time to think about lunch."

The sayyid and the mullah said, "No, dear uncle, we've eaten a lot of fruit and aren't hungry. We don't want to impose upon you. We really don't need to have any lunch."

The gardener turned to the sayyid and said, "Lord sayyid, I am the sacrifice of your ancestor. Our house is not far, but the noisy children won't let a man take a nap after lunch. It's better that since you are the youngest, you go to my house and tell them that the gardener says we are three persons. Tell them to give you our lunch. Bring whatever they give you here, and we'll eat it together. The house is not a long way off. Go left at the second lane. Knock on the fourth door on the right-hand side and say that you have come from the garden."

The gardener knew there was no one in the fourth house of that lane.

Taking his green shawl, the sayyid left to bring the lunch. Then the gardener moved closer to the mullah.

"Look, dear friend," the gardener said. "I have no problem with having a good respectable man such as yourself as my guest for a few days, but we should be fair about it. I am a hardworking gardener and you are a hardworking religious teacher. You teach the rules of prayer and fasting to the people. We have an obligation to you. Indeed, I feel indebted to you.

"But that sayyid is something else! Besides winding a green shawl around his head, what else can he do? What is his benefit to the people that he should be such a professional freeloader? And it isn't certain that he really is a descendant of the Prophet. Maybe his green shawl is a lie! Such persons give the Prophet and imams a bad reputation. When did the Prophet ever say that his descendants should eat without paying? Your friendship with such people lowers you in the people's esteem.

"When he comes back I want to give him a piece of my mind! Please let me set matters straight between him and me and I'll send him on his way. Then your excellency can spend one month during the heat of summer here. I can learn some rules of religion from you and you may relax. You see, I can understand why I should make you my guest, but I don't know what right that sayyid has to stay in my garden and ruin my life!"

The mullah, eager for the one-month's hospitality in the delightful garden, said, "You are right, but, of course..."

"There are no 'buts,'" said the gardener. "You don't do anything. I'll arrange things myself!"

Meanwhile the sayyid had followed the gardener's instructions and knocked on the door. No one answered, so he returned empty-handed to the garden and said, "There was no one home."

"Okay," said the gardener sharply. "So there wasn't anyone at home. Do you know what, Mr. Sayyid? The more I think about it, I can see that this shaykh is an old friend, and I want spend more time with him and talk about things. It's best if you pick up that basket of grapes and leave us right now. You're not needed here; depart in peace!"

The sayyid looked at the mullah and saw that his companion avoided his glance and would not speak on his behalf. Then he realized that the gardener had done his work well and had tempted the mullah. So the sayyid said to the mullah, "Very good, I shall go too. But, Mr. Mullah, it is against the rules of friendship that we arrive together and I leave alone while you remain dumb!"

"What can I say?" asked the mullah. "It's not my garden."

"That's why I said it," said the gardener. "Yes, the garden is mine and the mullah is my honored guest and my lord. It's nobody else's business. It was wrong for you to come here from the beginning. Now get out! If you don't, I know how to deal with you!"

"All right," said the sayyid, "but I can see that the mullah with all of his lordliness and old friendship won't see any good from this. God keep you; I'm on my way."

And so the sayyid started to leave. The gardener went after him and when they were a little way from the garden seized the sayyid by the neck and slapped him hard.

"You're very impudent! You enter a man's garden without permission and eat his property. And then you talk back! In truth, a baby camel is like a camel, and a lion cub is like a lion, but what resemblance do you have to the character of the Prophet? Did you your illustrious ancestor tell you to loaf around in idleness and extend your hand to people to take their goods without payment? Ya allah! Get away from this village as fast as you can, or I'll call the people and tell them about the way you have been acting. You'll lose every shred of respect and honor!"

So the sayyid went away, too.

As soon as the sayyid was out of sight, the gardener returned to the garden and locked the door firmly. With a large stick in his hand he went to the mullah and stood in front of him.

"Lord mullah!" he said. "Now is the time for settling accounts. Why don't you speak?"

"What should I say?" asked the mullah in surprise.

"Tell me by what right you entered this garden and stole my grapes, apples, and pears? I want to know in which book of religion is it written that one may enter someone's garden or house without permission and take the owner's property without his knowledge. In which book of religious rules or law is such a thing written? Ya allah! Answer me! If you don't, I'll beat you with this stick!"

The unfortunate mullah was dumbfounded at this turn of events.

"Such a thing is not to be found in any book," he said cautiously, "But, anyway, we were three persons and guests. I wasn't alone. I don't understand what your good humor at first was and what this bad humor is now!"

"At first you were three men," said the gardener. "If you had remained together you would all still be here. If each one of you had been alone, you would have been as you are now.

"You certainly weren't guests," the gardener added,

"because no one invited you here. And now you must agree with what I say. My first good humor was because I was alone and you had two other spongers as accomplices. And my bad humor now is because you are a sinner and I have a stick in my hand. When a person doesn't punish himself, then others must punish him. What do you say to that?"

"Nothing," said the mullah. "I have nothing to say. To tell the truth, I am not even a mullah! I bought this robe and turban with cash and on time so that I could live without paying for anything by wearing them. In fact, I am illiterate and wouldn't know a book of religious rules or law if I saw one! My friends were frauds like me. You have the right to do anything to me you want. Since I have lost my friends out of greed for sponging and freeloading, your strategy was a good one."

"If that's the way it is, take your medicine!" cried the gardener. He beat the wearer of cloak and turban with his stick and drove him out of the garden humiliated. He closed the gate behind him, sat down comfortably and lit his pipe. Puffing on it, he sent rings of smoke into the air.

9
THE WISE MAN AND THE FOOL

Once a man who had a good portion of knowledge and experience but few of the things of the world was traveling on foot from city to city. On the road he came upon an Arab riding astride two large sacks on the back of a camel. As the Arab rode, he sang.

The man on foot thought to himself, "Even though I am on foot and exhausted and the Arab is riding a camel and in good humor, I have at least found a fellow traveler. I'll be able to talk with him and pass the time faster. I'll make my long journey shorter with conversation and stories."

When he reached the camel rider, he greeted him with "Salam" and said, "I'm happy to meet you. I became very happy when I saw you. I was getting bored with loneliness, not to speak of the fatigue from trudging on foot. We'll be able to chat together for as long as we are traveling the same road."

"I was singing out of loneliness, too," said the rider. "It's the same whether you are on foot or riding. In fact, travel is better on foot. When you don't have a camel you don't have to worry about it. What you don't have will never get sick or stolen or run away. Even the poet says:

The person who doesn't have a donkey is comfortable,
He doesn't have to concern himself about its hay or
oats."

"What can I say?" asked the walker. "I don't think
that's right. If a person has something to carry but doesn't
have a donkey, why, then he has to carry it on his own
shoulders. If the road is long, he makes his feet sore. But,
well, I really don't dislike walking. When I remember that
I am bearing the burden of my own body, I feel happy. But
if I were riding a camel, I might suppose that the animal
beneath me was not happy with me."

The camel rider laughed. "That's something! People
who don't have camels think like that! God created camels
to carry loads and eat thorns. If you don't ride one, someone else will!"

The man on foot said, "In any case, you have a good
camel. God forgive you, it looks as though his load is very
heavy. What have you got in those sacks?"

"One of them is full of wheat I'm bring home from the
fields," answered the rider. "The other is full of sand and
gravel."

The walker was astonished. "What did you say? Full of
sand and gravel? Why are you taking that home? Can't
you find it in the city?"

"I'm not carrying the sand and gravel to use it," said
the rider. "I only had enough wheat to fill one of the sacks.
I couldn't load just one on one side of the beast, so I filled
the other with sand and gravel to balance the load. Then
too, I could also sit on the load."

Upon hearing this, the man on foot broke into laughter.
"What a marvelous arrangement you have made! Listen,

brother, instead of doing that, it would have better if you had divided the wheat into two parts and put a half in each of the sacks. Then you'd have a balanced load on both sides of the camel and you'd still have been able to ride on it. The load would be lighter for the camel and easier to put on and take off."

The camel-riding Arab was an ordinary fellow and not too smart. "Well done! Bravo! I was trying to figure out how to do it, but I couldn't. It's obvious that you are a very intelligent, wise, and great man."

"I don't know," said the other. "No, it was pretty simple, really."

The rider felt sorry for the man on foot and said to himself, "It would be better if I let this wise man ride."

Suddenly a thought occurred to him and he asked the walker, "Well, O great wise man, tell me the truth. Who are you? With such intelligence and understanding you must be a vizier at least! Or a deputy, a sultan, or a prince? You must be something big; you must be a very important man!"

"No," said the other. "I'm just an ordinary man like everyone else. And I'm not that learned. Look at the shape I'm in! My clothes are ordinary, like those of most folks."

"That can't be true!" protested the rider. "With your brains, you must have a lot of money to enjoy and to make you happy and carefree so that you could solve the problem of wheat so easily."

"As it happens," replied the walker, "I haven't got anything at all in this world. While I am now accompanying you, I haven't the faintest idea where I'll work tomorrow or what I'll eat."

"Naturally you have some shop or business," the camel

rider went on, "so if you don't have cash, you have a lot of goods. What's the difference? I mean, a learned man should have wealth and be fortunate. There was a poet who once said 'whoever has knowledge has power.'"

"Nothing like that," said the walker. "If I had a shop I would be sitting in it and doing business, and I certainly wouldn't be walking in this desert."

The rider nodded knowingly. "It's plain you don't want your identity to be made known, sir. Perhaps you have herds of camels and cattle and flocks of sheep and are going after your shepherds and herders. Anyway, a smart and sharp man such as you must have a flourishing business."

"Look, brother," sighed the other, "I don't have horses. I don't have camels. I don't have cattle. I don't have sheep. I don't have a shop or any money. I don't think I am unfortunate, but I simply don't have any worldly possessions. However, my body is strong and I work and I eat. I didn't find any work today, so I'm going to a nearby city to look for some. Of the understanding and intelligence that you are talking about, I have nothing. Just a simple life; that's all there is to it."

"Then you are a lazy good-for-nothing! A pauper!" cried the rider. "Here I am with a sack of wheat and a sack of sand! In spite of my illiteracy and lack of wits I own dozens of camels, hundreds of sheep, and fifty cows. I own two farms, a granary. I have maids and servants. I have honor and esteem. I have shoes and clothes. I have ten rooms full of household goods. When I go to a meeting, I am respected and saluted. I have a comfortable life. I am member of the city reform committee. In my house I have a room full of books which is the envy of the local mullah. I have gotten all of this through my dull wits!"

He continued contemptuously, "Now, you who clever enough to know how to load wheat on a camel, what do you have? So, what's the good of your intelligence, understanding, and experience? If that is intelligence, nothing but imagination and trouble, then I want no part of it! As it happens, I need a laborer on one of my farms, but I'm afraid to hire the likes of you. Hurry up! Get away from me! I'm afraid your misfortune will afflict me. Useless intelligence is bad luck!"

"I'm going," said the man on foot, "but with all that you've said, in my opinion you're a miserable, stupid fool. All the things that you have, you've bought with money while you're still a dolt! I would never want to be like you!"

So the man on foot left the man on the camel and went on his way. As it happened, the camel rider traveled some distance when he met up with two more men on camels. They were bandits and the asked him what he had in his sacks.

"Just now there was a man with me who went that way," he answered. "He said that I was a miserable fool. That's what I am and whatever is in the loads is what it is."

One of the bandits took out his knife and slit one of the sacks. It happened to be the one containing the sand and gravel. As a result the bandits beat him and then went away, saying, "What a strange, stupid fellow! The desert is full of sand and you load sand on your camel?"

But the Arab camel rider whose sack of wheat had escaped the thieves by this chance, smiled happily. "God bless my stupidity," he said to himself. "If I hadn't loaded the sand and gravel, I would have lost the wheat!"

After this, people observed that that man would load even a hundred camels with one sack of wheat and the other of sand. He wouldn't listen to anyone or take anyone's advice. Instead, he would say to those who laughed at his stupidity, "I know something that you don't know."

The poor man became a laughing-stock, but in his heart he was satisfied that he knew something which they didn't know. And he had camels and farms and everything.

. .

10
A PRACTICAL LESSON

Once there was a merchant who had a talking parrot that he had placed in a cage. The parrot would entertain the merchant with its talk.

Things were thus until one day the merchant decided to travel to India. When he had made ready and was about to depart, he asked his family, his servants, and his maids what present he should bring back for them. Each of them had a request. One wanted a Kashmiri shawl, another a peacock. Still another wanted an ivory comb. Other requests were for a bottle of sugar, medicinal ointment, and a list of spices such as cardamom, cinnamon, ginger, pepper, plus many other things besides.

The merchant wrote them all down dutifully and then went to the parrot to say good-bye to he bird. He asked the parrot, "What do you want from India?"

"I want your safety and good health. I don't want any presents, but I have heard that there are many parrots in India. My desire is that when you reach India and have passed through its luxuriant, green forests and have seen the Indian parrots flying happily about, that you greet them on my behalf and say, 'My parrot wants instructions from you. He sends this message, that the condition of friendship and brotherhood is that you think of me. I, too, would like to be happy as you are.'

> How is it just that I remain confined
> While you fly from meadow to tree?

"Just give them my message and bring me their answer," added the parrot. "I want nothing else."

The merchant agreed to do as the parrot asked and wrote that down, too. He promised to deliver the message and to bring back the reply of the Indian parrots.

After he had reached India, one day he rode a horse out to see the jungle. He found several beautiful and sweet-voiced parrots there in the glades and trees flying joyfully about. The merchant remembered the request of his parrot and reined his horse to a halt. He called the parrots and delivered his parrot's message and asked what answer they wanted him to take back.

But as soon as the merchant had finished repeating the message, one of the Indian parrots shuddered and fell unconscious from the bough of the tree to the ground. The others remained silent and did not answer the merchant.

He was astonished at this. He wanted to keep his promise to his parrot, so he tried to get their reply again. "O parrots! What's this? My parrot is of your kind and is waiting for your answer. Please give him your reply."

Again, one of the parrots fell to the ground from the tree and fainted. The other parrots stayed silent and said nothing.

Seeing the tragic reaction of the birds to his words, the merchant regretted what he had done and blamed himself.

"What a monstrous thing I have done!" he said to himself. "I described the sadness of my parrot and caused the death of these parrots. I really didn't think that they might be related to my parrot or that they would fall senseless from the pain and memory of their separation and forget how to speak in their sorrow for him."

But nothing could be done about that now, so there was nothing for the merchant to do but leave that place. After that he spoke no more to the Indian parrots about his parrot's message and resumed his travels. He completed his buying and selling and set out for his own country with his profits and the presents he had bought for the members of his household.

When he was back home and had finished distributing the gifts, he went to the parrot.

"Dear friend," said the parrot. "You've brought presents for everybody. Where is the good news that you were to bring to me? What did you say to the parrots and what was their reply?"

"Beloved parrot," said the merchant sadly, "I gave them your message, but I am sorry that I did. If I had known what would happen, I wouldn't have done it, because when they heard my words they became very sad and would not give an answer."

"That's not possible!" cried the parrot. "I know parrots. It isn't possible that they wouldn't reply! Parrots are better-natured than humans and more faithful. If you had given them my message they certainly would have given an answer!"

The merchant shook his head. "It's just the way I told you. We'd better forget about this matter now. I'll arrange for anything you want."

"I don't want anything else," cried the parrot. "I just want to know what they said and what they did when you gave them my message."

"As long as you insist," said the merchant, "I have to tell you that they didn't utter a single word at all, but when I gave them your message containing your complaints and the verse you'd recited, one of the parrots got upset and became very sad. He trembled and fell to the ground from the branch of the tree and the others didn't say anything.

"I was obliged to repeat my words and again ask for a reply. At that, another of the birds fainted and fell to the ground while the others still said nothing. When I realized that they were not going to answer, I was sorry that my words had caused the death of that parrot. I don't know; perhaps they were your relatives, maybe they weren't. But I know this. Not one of them said anything that I could understand."

When the merchant had reached this point in his story, the parrot understood the meaning of the Indian parrots' behavior. He squawked loudly, trembled, and fell motionless to the floor of his cage.

The merchant was appalled at this spectacle and became even more remorseful. He didn't understand what had happened, but in any case, his parrot lay still; sorrow and regret would be useless.

So, he opened the door of the cage to check whether there was still any sign of life in his pet. Finding none, he took off the little chain that tied the parrot's foot to his cage and threw the bird outside onto the grass. He was saddened by the whole business of the message and what had followed from it.

But the parrot, as soon as it found itself free from the cage, flapped its wings and took flight and flew to the branch of a nearby tree.

The merchant was dumbfounded at this turn of events. He looked up and asked the bird, "What is this that I see you doing? Why? Now that you are in a tree you can fly away whenever you want to, but first you must tell where you learned such a trick! I fulfilled my promise by delivering your message, so you must tell me the truth."

"You humans learn nothing from advice!" declared the parrot. "You get no benefit from what you hear or what you read in books. But we parrots, we understand a practical lesson better than mere words and we learn from it.

"As you are a good man and delivered my message honestly and brought back their answer correctly, I will tell you the truth. In my message I described my problem and asked the parrots of India for a solution. They gave it by a practical lesson. First, by remaining silent they told me that the reason for my confinement was the sweetest of my voice. The solution to that was silence.

"Next, one or two of the parrots fell unconscious. In that was a practical lesson in which they were saying that if you are a seed the chickens will eat you. If you are prey, the hunter will hunt for you. However, as you don't have claws and fangs and are imprisoned in a cage, you must become useless, worn out, silent, unconscious, and helpless. Then they will no longer want you. Then you will become free!

"The peacock is a prisoner because of its beauty, the parrot because of its speech. My beauty and my sweet words were my downfall. The Indian parrots told me that I must be silent and become nothing in order to become alive again and free.

"This was the practical lesson that they gave me. Now you see that I have done what they taught me, and now I am free!"

So, saying "Peace (*salam*)," the parrot flapped its wings and flew off towards the far horizon.

11
AN HONEST, THOROUGH JOB

Sultan Mahmud had a slave named Ayaz of whom he was very fond. In ancient times slavery was common; prisoners captured in war were often taken to cities and sold to be servants and maids. Until someone freed them for the love of God, they were had to work and serve their masters. They could be bought and sold like animals. Some spent their entire lives as slaves; while others, who had some skill or knew some useful kind of work and were smart and intelligent, would gradually work their way into the favor of their masters and achieve honor and power.

Ayaz was a black youth who had been taken prisoner in battle and had been sold several times in various cities until it happened that he was taken into the royal court of Sultan Mahmud of Ghaznah. There his intelligence, quick wit, and integrity attracted the attention of the king. Gradually he became one of the Mahmud's closest friends and confidants.

However, since Ayaz was always with the king, and the king favored him very much, naturally there were others who became jealous of him and said things such as: "What does this mean? Why does the king like a black slave so much? Why does the king allow him to interfere in everything? Why does he put Ayaz in charge of other servants and workers?"

Because their envy blinded them to Ayaz's good qualities, they gossiped and made accusations declaring Ayaz unfit for such favor. But Sultan Mahmud had tested the intelligence and honesty of Ayaz again and again, and the youth had demonstrated many times that he was more worthy then any of the others.

As an example, it is said that one day Mahmud and his retinue were riding their horses on a road. Ayaz was with them. They came to a desert. While they were riding rapidly, an idea struck Mahmud, so he took the large purse of money that he had with him and, without looking back, began to throw handfuls of coins onto the ground over his shoulder as he rode.

After a few minutes, Sultan Mahmud looked back and saw that every one of his companions had stopped to pick up the money. Except Ayaz, who was still with him.

"Where is the retinue?" Mahmud asked Ayaz.

"They're coming behind us," Ayaz answered. "I think they are busy picking up the money."

"Why didn't you stop with them," demanded Mahmud. "Why did you stay with me?"

"They saw gold and forgot service," said Ayaz, "but my duty is my service to you, and I am at your service."

"What?" cried Mahmud. "When you see that my lawful property is strewn on the ground and will be lost? Shouldn't you have been concerned about that?"

"Of course I was," said Ayaz. "If your purse had had a hole in it and you didn't know that the coins were falling out of it, I would have called your attention to it. But when I saw you throwing the money deliberately onto the ground, I thought that there must be some reason for what the king is doing."

"What? Is it possible to have a reason for throwing money away in the desert?"

Ayaz shrugged. "Anyway, I know that since my king is an intelligent man, why isn't it possible? For instance, when an enemy is following someone, the greed for the money would slow the enemy down and increase the distance between them."

"But if no enemy were following?"

"At least," said Ayaz, "the faithfulness of friends may be made known."

After several such incidents and tests, Ayaz became more and more a favorite of the king.

And so it happened that one day the sultan decided to go on a hunt.

Sultan Mahmud summoned twenty of his princes and courtiers and said, "Prepare yourselves for tomorrow we shall go on a hunt."

The next day, as the royal party left the city, the princes and commanders noticed that Ayaz was traveling close beside the king. They didn't like that. They grumbled among themselves, saying, "The king takes that worthless servant everywhere with him, even on a hunt. But every one of us is wiser and smarter than Ayaz. We are princes and commanders and serve the king better than he does. We are stronger than he is in battle. What good is such a slave on a hunt anyway?"

Finally they chose one their number to present their complaints about Ayaz to the king. The representative was to tell the king that the favor he was showing Ayaz was an insult to the commanders. Even if Ayaz was better for service in the palace, he was to say, others were quicker and more suitable than he in the desert!

So their designated representative spurred his horse forward and received permission to approach the king so that he might deliver the message of the commanders.

"The commanders say, your majesty," he said, "if we knew that there was a justification for the favor of your majesty to Ayaz, perhaps others would not be upset. But this favor and honor has no good basis and it weakens the motivation and loyalty we should all have in your majesty's service. We are the ones who do battle. We are the ones who hunt. We are the ones who undertake important works and complete them. We protect your majesty from every harm. And then we see this Ayaz lording himself over us, and that without just cause!"

Sultan Mahmud said, "All right. If that is the situation, let's make a test. Then it will become clear. If I am making a mistake, I should know it. If I am right, then let there be no more complaints. Let the cause of my favor be demonstrated."

Then Mahmud ordered a halt. He pointed out a tree in a field on the right to Ayaz. "Listen, Ayaz. Do you see that tree? Go quickly to the foot of that tree and stand facing it until I summon you with the sound of clashing swords and spears. Then put your sword under the tree and come back to me."

"As you command," said Ayaz. Leaving the king and the commanders, he spurred his horse to the tree. He dismounted from his horse and waited under the tree.

Sultan Mahmud gathered the prices and commanders

around himself.

"Today," he said, "with your help we will solve a problem. If I've made a mistake in my judgment, we can correct it."

"The king has but to command us," the men replied.

"Listen well. In my eyes you are all valuable and honorable. You are all equal. In order to make this discussion easier, you must choose one man from among yourselves, one whom you all trust and whose judgment and truthfulness you believe in, so that we can finish this affair speedily."

"The king has but to command."

So they talked it over and selected the same man who had delivered their message to the king. He was older than the others and all had confidence in his integrity and good will.

The king said to him, "Now that you are the representative of twenty nobles, come let us have a space of about fifty paces between us and the rest of the group and we may begin."

So the rest of the men moved away fifty paces and waited.

Then Sultan Mahmud whispered to the representative, "Look! There is a caravan moving along that road in the distance. I'd like to know where it is coming from. Go there quickly and bring me the information."

So the man rushed to the caravan and asked the leader of the caravan. Then he rode back faster than could be thought possible and reported to the king:

"May your majesty live long in good health! The caravan is coming from Khorasan."

"Didn't you learn where it was going?"

"No, your majesty, I didn't ask."

"Very good. Stay with me."

Then the king summoned another of the commanders and said, "Do you see that caravan? Go and find out where it is going."

That man went to the caravan as fast as he good and asked where it was going. Then he rushed back to the king and said, "It is going from Khorasan to Madinah in Hejaz."

"Didn't you find out how many persons were in the caravan?" asked the king.

"No, your majesty, I didn't ask."

"Very good," said the king. "Stay here."

The king called a third man and said, "Do you see that caravan? I want to know how many persons are in it. Go as quickly as you can and bring me the information."

So the third commander went and returned.

"Good health to your majesty!" he said as he saluted. "There are 180 persons in the caravan. They are coming from Khorasan and traveling to Hejaz."

"Didn't you learn whether they were travelers or merchants?"

The man shook his head. "I didn't ask."

"Very good," said the king. "Stay here."

Then Mahmud called a fourth man. "Do you see that caravan? It is coming from Khorasan and going to Hejaz. Get there as fast as you can and ask whether the people in it are common travelers or merchants and, if so, what they are carrying."

The man obeyed and rushed immediately to the caravan and brought back the information that most of the men in it were merchants taking stone pots, silk cloth, carpets, pistachio nuts, almonds, and other things from

Khorasan to Hejaz.

"Didn't you learn what day they set out from Khorasan and how many days it took to get this far?"

"No, your majesty. I didn't ask."

"Very good," said the king. "Stay here at my side."

And so the king summoned the rest of the princes and commanders one by one and sent each one with a question and each one returned with the answer to it adding to the general information.

Then Sultan Mahmud said to them, "Now, let's get to the point. The man you selected first is here as are the rest of you. You have seen what was done. Now, strike your swords and spears together so that the noise may bring Ayaz."

They did as the king commanded. Ayaz, still waiting under the tree and not having heard or seen any of what had passed between the king and his commanders, heard the signal and hung his sword on the tree. He rode back to the group. In their presence, Mahmud said to Ayaz, "Ayaz, do you see that caravan moving along the road in the distance? I want to know where if came from and where it is going. Hurry up and bring the information so that we can move on."

Ayaz spurred his horse but took a little more time than the others had before he returned.

"Good health to your majesty!" he said upon return. "The caravan is coming from Khorasan and traveling to Hejaz."

"Didn't you learn how many persons there were in it?" asked the king.

"I did. In it there are 170 men and two women."

"Didn't you learn whether they were travelers or merchants?"

"I asked," said Ayaz. "A few of them were travelers going on the pilgrimage to Makkah, but most were merchants."

"It would have been a good if you had asked about the goods they were carrying to Hejaz," said Sultan Mahmud.

"I did ask," said Ayaz. "The were carrying bolts of silk cloth, Khorasani rugs, stone vessels and plates, pistachio nuts, almonds, and dried fruits."

"Didn't you learn what day the caravan set out?"

"Certainly, your majesty. They set out on the 7th of Rajab and they have been on the road two months. They stopped for a week in Rayy to buy and sell."

Sultan Mahmud asked Ayaz a few more things about the caravan and Ayaz gave him the answers. Then the king said, "Very good, where is your sword?"

"I hung it on that tree," Ayaz said.

"Go bring your sword. We want to get on our way."

When Ayaz was at a distance, Sultan Mahmud said to his commanders, "I must speak. You asked about the reason for my friendship and you have seen the result of the test I put to you and to him. You are twenty commanders and Ayaz is but one, a black slave. I sent you one by one on a task of which Ayaz knew nothing. Yet the answers you brought back were incomplete and deficient. You could have found out everything he found out, but you did not. You just brought back the answer to my question. I don't want to criticize any of you. You have many fine skills that Ayaz does not have. You can do many things he cannot do. But the things that he can do and is capable of doing, he does honestly and thoroughly. Is there a need for any further explanation?"

The representative of the commanders said, "I bear witness that your majesty is right. A person who does his job honestly and thoroughly, no matter how small and insignificant it may be, no matter who he is, or where he is, will be loved and favored. And he should be!"

12
AN UNFAIR VERDICT

Once there was a weak, skinny old man who was very sick. He went to a doctor and said, "I'm very ill. Do something!"

The doctor took his pulse and examined his tongue. Then he asked, "What did you eat last night?"

"Nothing."

"What did you have for breakfast?" asked the physician.

"Nothing."

The doctor saw that not only was the old man sick, but he was also starving and spiritless. It was as though he were about to collapse and pass away from lack of food and energy. The man of medicine felt sorry for the old man. In order not to increase his anxiety, the doctor said, "Do you know that your illness doesn't need any special diet or medicine? In order to get better, you should do want you want. Eat whatever you like and do whatever you like. If you do that, you'll get better."

"What you say is right," said the sick man, "but the fact is I can't eat anything I want to eat. I don't have the means to do that."

The doctor felt even more pity for him. Since he did not want to increase the old man's discomfort at the end of his life, he said, "I meant that you shouldn't think about such things. Anyway, you should enjoy life as much as you are able. You should fulfill your dreams as much as you can. Eat as much as you can so that you can do what you feel like doing."

"God bless you, doctor! God bless you, for you have made me feel better. I knew that my whims and wishes have never been realized."

"Yes, my good man," said the doctor. "That's it! May God make you well! Now, go wherever you want and fulfill your dreams."

"I want to go and look at meadows and flowing water," said the old man.

"Excellent!" said the doctor. "Go in good health!"

So the old man, pleased with the doctor's advice, walked to some meadows and by a river admiring the scenery as he went. When he had gone a little way he saw a dervish sitting on the river bank. The dervish was bent over the river washing his face and hands.

The sick man looked at the back of the dervish's neck and saw that it was clean and smooth. A perfect spot for a slap! He felt a sudden urge to strike the dervish there. He knew that he shouldn't hit another man without reason, but he recalled the doctor's words, that the remedy for his condition was to do whatever he wanted to do and surrender to his whims.

The old man was unable to fight the impulse. He rolled up his sleeve, got closer, aimed at the back of the dervish's head, raised his hand, and slapped him hard on his ear.

When the old man heard the sound of the blow, he began to laugh.

The dervish, who had been busy washing his face and hands, managed not to fall into the water with great difficulty. He shouted in outrage at the blow and jumped up to grab his assailant and beat him up. But when he looked at the sick man who appeared to be at death's door, he realized that if he took revenge, it might result in the old man's death. So he seized his hand and said:

"Wretch! Don't you want to keep your head on your body? Why did you hit me without any provocation? You haven't got the strength to hit me hard, and you are too weak for me to hit you. Why did you do it? Why are you laughing like that? Are you crazy?"

"I don't know why I did it," said the sick man. "I just felt the urge and the doctor had told me to. As for my laughing, that was because the slap made a strange sound and I knew that it didn't know whether it was from my hand or your neck."

"You don't know?" cried the dervish. "I'll explain it to you now!"

The dervish took the sick man's hand and dragged him to the house of the judge. He described what had happened and finished up, saying, "And that is my complaint. Now, here is the culprit and you are the judge. If you say that I should retaliate, then say so and I'll to it. If not, what is to be done? I was afraid to hit him because he is so weak I might kill him. In any event it isn't right that in a city where there is a judge that a man should strike another without cause."

The judge looked at the sick man and knew that he could not order the dervish to hit him in retaliation as it could cause his death. So he cautioned the dervish, saying, "Friend, you can't hit this sick old man because he might die and then his blood would be on your head. Beating and imprisonment is just for strong, healthy men, not for such as he. He's barely alive as it is. Come, forgive him. They say that there is a pleasure in forgiveness that is not to be found in revenge. Forgiveness is appropriate in a situation like this."

"Why should I forgive him?" demanded the dervish angrily. "What sort of an unfair verdict are you delivering? If people hear about it, there will be no stopping anyone! For every crime there must be a punishment! I'll never forgive him, not for thirty years! You must punish him!"

The judge shook his head. "It is as I've said. This man is ill and sick. He's on the point of death. You must withdraw your complaint."

"I'll never agree to such a thing!"

The judge turned to the sick man. "Look, how much money have you got?"

"Nothing."

"What did you eat this morning?"

"Nothing."

"Do you see?" said the judge to the dervish. "He's also hungry! His slap hasn't taken anything from you. Let him go. How much money do you have?"

"Six dirhams," said the dervish.

"Good," said the judge. "Divide the money in half and give three dirhams to this sick man so that he may go to get something to eat. God will reward you for it."

"What a strange predicament I've fallen into!" protested the dervish. "I am slapped by him and I should pay him? This is unjust! It's tyranny and compulsion. What kind of a judgment are you giving? How much does each slap cost?"

The judge and the dervish started to argue. While they were doing so, the sick old man was thinking. "It's clear that one slap is worth three dirhams."

His eye fell on the nape of the judge's neck and saw that it was brighter, smoother, and nicer than the dervish's. Once again he felt the urge. While the dervish and the judge were still shouting at each other, he raised his hand and boxed the judge's ear as hard as he could, crying, "Now you give me three dirhams, too, to make things even!"

At this turn of events, the judge was very upset, but the dervish was delighted. He took out his six dirhams and said to the judge, "Take them. Three dirhams for the blow he struck on me and the three for the blow he struck on you!"

"What are saying?" cried the judge. "Are you paying to have me beaten?"

"Yes," replied the dervish. "If a box on the ear is right for one, it is right for all. If it is wrong for one, it is wrong for all. It's too bad I don't have any more money on me. If I had, I would have paid a hundred dirhams for him to hit you again. That would be right and just for such an unfair verdict! Then you might learn that whatever you don't approve of for yourself you shouldn't approve of for others."

13
MOSES AND THE SHEPHERD

One day Moses was walking along a road. Suddenly he heard a heartbreaking sound from off the side of the road. When he went to see where the sound was coming from, he found a simple-hearted shepherd behind a hill who was baring his soul to God.

"O my Lord," he was saying, "if I knew where You were, I would come myself and serve You. I'd comb Your hair, I'd sew Your shoes, I'd wash Your clothes. O God! I am Your friend. If I could see You, I would sacrifice myself for You. I would give You all of my goats and sheep. O God! I want to know where You are so that I can bring You yogurt and cheese and bread and oil and milk. I'd come to You every day and do whatever You wanted done. I'd sweep Your house. If You got sick, I'd take care of You. . ."

He continued in this vein while Moses grew outraged at the shepherd's words. He went up to him and shouted at him:

"You impudent fool! Why do you talk such nonsense? You're talking heresy. Such words are a sin! Such words are very wrong! You must repent and never say things like that again. Hurry up and close your mouth. Don't say another thing!"

"Who are you?" asked the shepherd. "What is it to you? I'm not saying anything bad and I'm not doing anything wrong. I am simply praying to my God and worshipping Him. I believe in God. Don't you believe in Him?"

"How can I not be a worshipper of God?" demanded Moses. "I teach the knowledge of God to mankind. I'm not telling you that you shouldn't worship God, but the God Whom we worship does not have a house. He doesn't have a special place. He doesn't have a body of flesh. He doesn't have a mortal soul. He doesn't use clothing. He doesn't have hands and feet. He doesn't have a head or a stomach. He doesn't eat food. He doesn't need anything! The things which you have been saying are what the unbelievers say who are outside of the faith. God doesn't have a need for anything!"

The shepherd was frightened and became ashamed. "Then what kind of a man is this God, may I be His sacrifice, that He doesn't need anything and doesn't want anything?"

Moses said, "God is not a man and is not like a man. God is unique, above and greater than everything else! He is like sense and intelligence and knowledge, none of which can be seen by the eye. He is everywhere. He is joined with nothing and is separate from nothing. He is all-powerful and all-knowing. All things are at His command. And this is the God Whom we worship."

"I don't understand such things," said the unlearned shepherd. "I love God and I am His sacrifice. I want to go and see Him and serve Him and wipe the dust from His feet on my eyes. Tell me the truth, who are you that you want me to be afraid of God?"

"I am Moses, the prophet of God. God wants me to do my job well. If you wish to serve God, do good to mankind and injure no one. God wants this; he doesn't want anything for Himself. No one can see God. You must repent for the words you have spoken and never say such things again. Such words are a sin and I fear that what you have been saying will excite God's wrath against you. A terrible calamity will fall from heaven; fire will come and people will be burned up. If you say such things one more time, you will be an unbeliever and God will not like you."

"Moses," cried the shepherd, "you've made me despair and you've sealed my lips. Your words have burned my soul. I'm afraid and I don't know what to do. Alas! How miserable I am!"

So the shepherd, in fear and regret, began to beat his head with his own hands and tear his clothes. He sighed and turned his face away from Moses and went off into the desert weeping.

Moses, too, at the result of this encounter was troubled and fell into thought. How can one teach simple-hearted folk about the One God? He was still pondering this problem when he received a revelation from God, saying, "O Moses, you have separated Us from of Our servants with this behavior. You are a prophet so that you may bring people closer to Us, not to make them despair. O Moses, We want the people to remember God and to be hopeful. The educated may speak better, but the simple-hearted, too, must worship God. People must do good. Everyone doesn't know how to speak well, but if the heart is with God, that is sufficient. We have sent you to invite mankind to God and to enlighten their hearts with the light of faith. Whatever that shepherd may have been, he was Our friend and had turned to Us. But you have broken his heart, O Moses. . ."

It was as though it had been said to Moses: "O Moses, there are people in the world who believe in the unseen God and who understand prophethood and sacred books, but there are also people who worship statues, snakes, calves, and other things that weary the human mind instead of the true God. The task is to first guide these lost ones towards God, and not to injure the feelings of God's worshippers while neglecting the idol worshippers."

At that moment Moses was deeply regretted what he had said to the shepherd. The fire of shame burned in his soul. He ran after the shepherd, following on the road that the shepherd was traveling as fast as he could. When he caught up with him, he said, "O shepherd, be glad, for God has sent down a command. I was too severe with you and there is no longer any problem:

Do not seek any rules or arrangements,
Say whatever your lonely heart desires.

Be with God and remember God in every way. Praise God with any words, God will accept them. He knows their truth and is pleased with the purity of your heart."

"O Moses," said the shepherd, "it is too late. I've suffered so much from regret that I've learned what I didn't know. God, Who knows all things, knows the state of my heart better than all others. I know that my heart is with God and it is not sinful. And if my tongue is unable to utter beautiful words, I'll cut short my speech. I have nothing else to say now. Peace!"

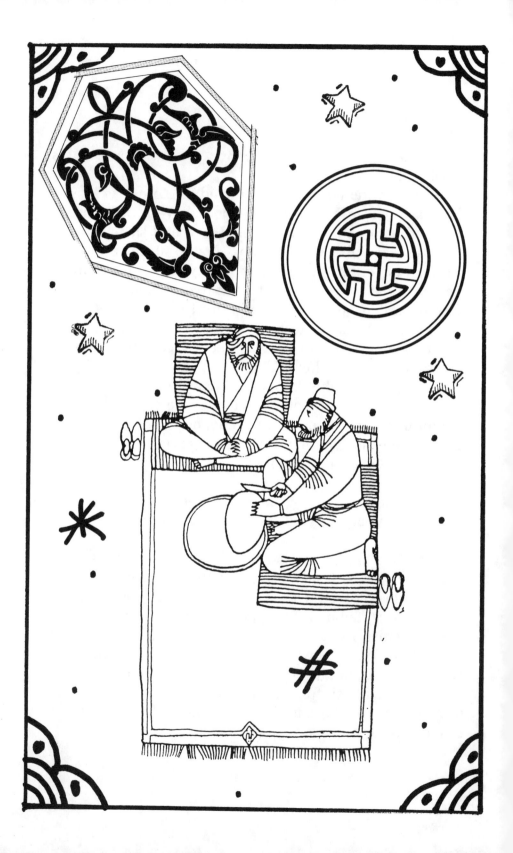

14

Luqman's Gratitude

Luqman the Wise was a thin, swarthy man who spent his entire life in learning from the example of others and giving counsel. In his own lifetime his intelligence, common sense, and wise words were famous in his country. Afterwards, his fame spread everywhere and he was remembered for his goodness, so much so that many considered him a prophet.

Among Luqman's words of counsel that have been recorded in books are these given to his son: "My dear son, when eating, always try to eat the best kinds of food; when sleeping, sleep in the best bedchamber; as long as you live, partake of the best pleasures that life offers. Wherever you go, build a house and pass your time in happiness with friends."

"Dear father," said his son, "what you say is not possible for me. The best food, bedchambers, and pleasures belong to the rich who can provide everything for themselves and build houses where they want. But I may not have wealth."

"That is the point," said Luqman. "People mostly imagine that the good things of life are bought with money, but that is wrong. A lot of money carries with it a lot of problems if it is not accompanied with intelligence. The very rich man spends his life in bitterness constantly trying to add to his wealth more so as to enjoy it even more! But there is no pleasure in money. Rather, pleasure is in the wisdom of life and happiness is in a peaceful mind.

"I'm not telling you to buy the most expensive food stuffs, or the softest bedding, or to take the most beautiful woman as your wife, or to build a house with bricks of crystal, gold, or silver.

"I'm saying try to live better and happier and to understand the meaning of life. To do that, it is enough to wait to eat until you are really hungry. Then the simple food that you eat will be like the finest delicacy. It is enough to work a little more and to sleep less to enjoy a good, refreshing rest. It will be as though you were sleeping in the most luxurious of beds. It is enough not to accustom yourself to continuous pleasure but to work hard and diligently and to think about the misfortunes of others in order to make the pleasures of your life sweeter and more enjoyable and to love life more. And it is enough to be beloved by people for goodness, kindness, and charity. Then, every place will be your home and the house of friendship may be built anywhere."

And Luqman told him many other useful things.

One of the incidents of Luqman's life remembered by others was that once he was taken prisoner and sold to an important man. The more this great personage observed Luqman's work, the more he was impressed by his slave's intelligence, sense, wisdom, knowledge, and faith. He became fond of Luqman and respected him.

Gradually things proceeded to the point that Luqman's master began to love him as though he were his son or brother and to treat him as though he were a companion and confidant. On every occasion, the master showed his servant Luqman honor and respect and offered the most choice morsels of food to him at meals as a sign of his affection.

Things were thus when a melon was brought to the master, a first fruit from his fields. He took a knife and cut a slice which, instead of eating himself, he offered to Luqman. Luqman took it and ate it. It was apparent from the expression on his face that it satisfied him. This pleased the master and he cut another piece and offered it to Luqman. Out of courtesy, Luqman accepted it and ate it as though he relished it. Then he thanked the great man.

This increased his master's delight, so he cut still another piece and gave it to Luqman. He continued doing this until there was only one slice left. The master said to himself, "Now I can eat a piece of this first fruit melon myself."

But when he ate it, he realized that the melon was spoiled and very bitter. His tongue and throat burned from the bitterness and he got very upset. He washed out his mouth and after a while said to Luqman:

"Dear friend, that melon was incredibly bitter and I didn't know it. How is that you didn't say anything about its bitter taste? Such patience is very difficult!"

"Yes," answered Luqman, "the melon was very bitter, but for some time I have received much sweetness from your hands and I didn't want to complain of the one-time bitterness of the melon. You have held me dear and I have held you dear. I always advise people that they must be grateful for the goodness of others. How could I not follow my own advice? I wish that you had given me that last piece so that you might have been happy with this show of your affection, just as I am satisfied and happy with your goodness and generosity."

15

THE IMAGINARY ILLNESS

Once there was a teacher who ran an old-fashioned primary school. He taught its thirty pupils how to read the Holy Quran and other books. The students would arrive at the school early, bringing their lunches with them, and stay until evening doing their lessons. They had no chance to play except on Fridays.

In the old days there were no grade or high schools like those we have today. In the old-fashioned primary schools, children would start with learning the alphabet and memorizing parts of the Holy Quran. They would learn to read and write and study some works of literature. When they had finished, they would either go about their business or trade, or enter a religious school to continue their studies in Arabic and the religious sciences. In those school there was no such things as a special hour for relaxation, play, or exercise; nor were there summer or winter vacations. The course of studies was serious and difficult with little opportunity for fooling around.

Besides that, the mullah in charge could strike misbehaving or slow students. The boys couldn't laugh or talk loudly. As they were being trained to be polite, the teacher was very severe. There is a famous verse about this:

If the teacher is too lenient,
The children will play games in the bazaar.

From this we can see that play and games were considered frivolous. Teachers would rage in school and
frighten their pupils with stern glances. They compelled
their students to pay strict attention. Thus, students
feared their teachers and showed them much respect. For
good or bad, that's the way things were!

Just the same, children in those days had a greater
interest in play and games and would grow tired of their
lessons. They looked forward to the Eid festivals and holi-
days. If the school was closed for a two- or three-day holiday, they would rejoice because they would at last find
some time for play.

So, in the quarter of the city where our story takes
place there were two such primary schools. One was called
the Shaykh's School, the other the Mullah's School.

One day one of the mullah's students was on his way to
school when he saw several of the students of the Shaykh's
School playing in the street. He asked why they weren't in
school.

"The shaykh is sick and the school's been closed for
three or four days," they replied.

The student went on to his school where the mullah
began to teach the class as usual. When the teacher left
the room on some errand, the student said to his class-
mates, "Have you heard the news?"

"What news?" they asked.

"The Shaykh's School is closed."

"Why?"

"The shaykh is sick."

"It's great for them that the shaykh is sick!" exclaimed the children. "But our teacher, Mr. Mullah, is firmly in his place. We'll never get a few days off."

But one of the students, shrewder than the others, said, "If you listen to me, I can make it so that we can have a few days off from school, too."

"Okay, but how?" the students asked.

"We'll make Mr. Mullah think that he's sick. . ."said the rogue.

"That's impossible!"

"Why? It's possible! I have a good plan, but it'll only work if we all agree to stick together and say the same thing. It's too late today to do anything today, but tonight I'll arrange things. Remember, we must all say the same thing! That's very important! Tomorrow we'll close the school, but today we'll have to do our lessons well so that the mullah will be pleased with us."

When the mullah returned the students recited their lessons much better than usual. In the evening, after the school had closed, the boys began to set their plan in motion for the next day.

Since the mullah's living quarters were next to the school, he usually arrived before any one else, but the students had agreed to gather at the school door early the next morning. The first to enter would be the most bold. He would be followed by ten more of the most audacious, one by one. They would set the plan into operation; then the rest of the students would go in together and say what they had agreed to say.

This was the plan: One by one they would say to the

mullah, "Sir! You seem pale. Aren't you well? I pray for your recovery." In that way, he would gradually think about being sick and become ill with an imaginary illness.

The next morning the students were gathered early at the school door. The cleverest among them entered first and as soon as his eyes fell upon the mullah, he said, "Sir, may God protect you from calamity! Why are you so pale? God forbid that you've become sick!"

The mullah replied, "No, it's nothing. Go to you place and start studying."

But the mullah began to think, "What did that mean? Have I become pale? I don't think so. Perhaps that's the way I appeared in this light. He's certainly mistaken!"

The second boy entered and greeted the mullah and then said, "Sir, it appears as though our teacher is not well today. I hope to God there is nothing wrong, but you seem to be very pale."

The mullah, who was the master of the school, said, "Thank you. Go and sit down."

He fell into thought, "the children can't be saying such things without reason."

He took the mirror from its niche and examined the color of his face in it, but he couldn't see anything unusual. Still, he began to think. . .

The third lad entered. After greeting the mullah, he said. "Mr. Mullah, God forbid, but why are you so pale today? Perhaps you've caught a cold. I hope you get well soon."

The mullah was gradually beginning to believe that his color was not normal. "Yes," he said, "I've caught a little cold. It's nothing. Go take your place."

The fourth student entered and greeted his teacher.

"Excuse me, sir, but you seem very pale and listless today. I hope it's not serious, but yesterday my father got like that. His head ached and he spent the whole day in bed."

"I don't know," said the mullah. "I'm tired. I've got a cold. I feel a little weak, but it's nothing to worry about. Go sit down and begin reading your lesson."

The mullah started thinking about headaches and soon he felt that his head was aching a little, but since he wasn't sick, he started work.

The fifth student entered, greeted the mullah, and said, "O my God! Sir! Why are you so pale? May God protect you! There are a lot of colds going about these days. Yesterday even my brother got sick. The doctor prescribed rest and he's better now."

The mullah was really feeling unwell now. It was as though his head was truly aching. He was seized with an overwhelming desire to lie down and rest.

The sixth boy, then the seventh, and then the eighth came in one after another, all saying about the same thing. Then the rest poured in together and all repeated the same thing.

Doubt began to gnaw at the mullah, and he was convinced that he was indeed ill. The idea gained strength in his mind. His voice trembled. He thought that he couldn't see clearly and his hands had lost their sense of touch. He thought: "Today all of the students look at me and say that I'm not well, but this morning my wife didn't say anything about my being pale and sick. What an uncaring wife I have! She doesn't think about my health at all!"

So he stood up and threw his cloak over his head and went to this own quarters. They were directly behind the school. He bawled out his wife, saying, "You can see that

I'm not well and don't even mention it! Other people's children are concerned about my welfare, but you don't care a thing about me!"

"I don't understand what you're talking about," she retorted. "You were perfectly fine this morning, and you still are as far as I can see!"

"Enough!" cried the mullah. "What a selfish woman! You don't think about me at all! It's a fact, all women lack common sense! You don't understand anything. The students, as small as they are, saw that I was sick, but you didn't! Hurry up and prepare my bed. I want to sleep. I'm dying from the pain!"

And because he had caught the imaginary illness and his head ached, he began to moan softly.

So the mullah went to bed. The children got wind of this and went to his room to enquire about him. The chief instigator said, "Now that things are thus, sir, if you give us permission, we'll stay right here with you and continue our studies."

They sat down in the shaykh's room around his bed and began to read aloud.

Then a couple of the rascals whispered to the first student, "This isn't right! We made the mullah sick and now we are still prisoners! You said that we would have a holiday!"

Said the clever lad, "Now we must gradually recite more loudly."

He made a sign and the boys began to read their lessons in loud voices. Speaking loudly enough for the shaykh to hear, he said, "Boys! Lower your voices. Be quiet for a time! This noise is harmful for our teacher. Noise is bad for a headache. Noise and commotion are not good for a sick man."

The mullah approved of these words and said, "You're right. In fact, now that I'm not in good shape today, get up and go! Take the day off and tomorrow we'll see how things are."

"Yes sir!" said the students trying to conceal their joy. "We hope that you get relief from your discomfort and get well very soon."

They took their leave and went out, very happy at the success of their trick.

When the children got home, their mothers asked them why they had come home so early. They replied, "The mullah is sick and he closed the school."

However some of the mothers did not believe their sons and they were afraid that their children were playing hooky from school. The boys replied: "It's easy to prove. Go and ask about the mullah's health!"

So a few of the mothers who were neighbors decided to make sure that their offspring were telling the truth. They went to the school to enquire about the condition of the mullah. They learned that, yes, the mullah was sprawled on his bed moaning and sighing about his headache. After doing that, the mother of the chief instigator of the trick said, "My husband is a doctor. I sent to him just now to come and bring some medicine."

As soon as the doctor arrived, he took the sick man's pulse and examined his tongue. He found no sign of illness in the mullah. He was forced to ask, "Sir, what are your symptoms?"

"My head aches," complained the mullah. "My body is numb. I'm in very bad shape. If you can, do something to cure the pain in my head. The rest isn't important. I'll sleep until I get better."

When a patient lies, he misleads the physician. Since he wasn't a psychic, the doctor had to take the sick man at his word. So the doctor wrote a prescription and prescribed a headache potion.

The medicine was brought, but as the mullah was not really sick, taking the medicine made things worse for him. And since the doctor had put him on a strict diet, he wasn't able to eat either. The result was that the mullah really became very sick and was forced to remain in bed for several days until he gradually began to recover.

It was several days before the mullah was able to reopen his school by which time the boys were tired of their games and the mullah was bored with his idleness and illness.

However, it is well-known saying that to hear the truth one must hear it from children. During the days of their holiday, wherever they went in order to show how clever they were they told their playmates the story of how they had made the mullah sick again and again. "The mullah wasn't sick; we made him sick!"

Their friends would ask, "How?"

They would say, "One day we made an agreement. Hasan said one thing, Husayn said the same thing, Rida said the same thing, and Mr. Mullah got sick from his imagination."

Eventually, the boys told the story to their parents in their homes. The women whispered it and finally the mullah's wife heard about it. She told her husband, and he realized that they had deceived him with suggestions and fancies. And he knew that the medicine taken when he wasn't truly sick had made him ill.

And so it happened that after that the mullah would never close the school when he was sick. He would appoint a substitute teacher! So the trick of the clever students ultimately worked to their own detriment.

16
THE MISUNDERSTANDING

One day four beggars from different countries who had recently become acquainted came to a village. One spoke Persian, another Turkish, the third Arabic, and the last spoke Greek. Though not one knew the tongue of any of the others, they managed to make their meaning known by means of sign language, mime, and a few common words. They learned from each other rapidly and whenever they got together and encountered something new they would ask each other in one fashion or another what the word for it was in their various languages. For example, the Persian might point to water and say "*ab*," the Arab "*mai*," the Turk "*su*," and so forth. Every day they came to learn a little more of each other's languages.

It was summer and the weather hot. A shared profession and the hardships of the road had made them close and they had agreed to meet in the afternoons and eat their midday meal together. So they would get together and eat whatever they had brought with them. Then they would sit in the shade for a while chatting. After that they would get up and go their separate ways.

One day, when they had spread the dining cloth on the ground, they discovered that each of them had brought bread and nothing else. The Persian said, "We aren't ungrateful, but it is hard to swallow dry bread. I don't have any money. If anyone has some, let him buy some fruit or something else to eat with the bread. Tomorrow someone else will make it up to him."

The other three said that they didn't have any money. "These villagers doesn't have much money," they complained. "There is bread and water, but they won't give anything else to a beggar."

So each one took a piece of bread and put it in his mouth. They were chewing on it without enthusiasm when a man passed by. He looked at the bare dining cloth and felt pity for the four beggars. He put his hand in his pocket, pulled out a coin, and tossed it onto the dining cloth.

The poor men prayed for the generous man and rejoiced. The Persian said, "Good! Here is the money; it belongs to all of us. Now, one of us should go and buy some *angur* with this coin to eat with the bread. I'm willing to go."

But the other three had not yet learned the meaning *angur*, and they protested. "No! *Angur* is no good. We should buy something that we all like. The money belongs to us all."

The Arab said, "Persian food is really rather tasteless. It's been a long time since I ate any *inab*."

No one other than the Arab had any idea what *inab* meant.

The Turk said, "Our Arab friend is always thinking Arab food. If you ask me, I say we spend the money uzum. That's cheap and good in the summer."

The Greek said, "No, no! I don't like Turkish food. Now that we have some money, it's better to get some *stafilia*. Please listen to me today. *Stafilia* is better than anything else.

"What kind of talk is this?" demanded the Persian. "One day is not a thousand days. I said that I have a yen for *angur* today. *Angur* isn't just a Persian food, it's everywhere. Besides, I'm the biggest and the oldest, so you should listen to what I say."

"The biggest!" cried the Arab. "So what? Is that a reason? A camel is big! But if you look at me, I'm the most learned. I know Arabic, and an Arab will never succumb to bullying!"

"Please!" said the Turk unhappily. "This is no place for a fight between an Arab an a Persian. And if there is going to be a fight, I'm stronger than anybody here and I'm not about to pay tribute to anyone! I said that we should have *uzum* today, if that's the way you feel about it, I won't eat anything more today!"

The Greek said, "Why are we talking like this? Let's go and change this coin for smaller ones and we can buy four kinds of food: some *angur*, some *inab*, some *uzum*, and I'll buy some *stafilia*. There's no reason to get upset."

"No," said the Arab. "We won't agree with any of your European ideas. We have just recently gotten to know each other, and now that we are together, we should have unity and agreement. If each one goes after his own fancy, then disputes will arise. In my opinion, today we can have inab, tomorrow something else."

"Aha!" cried the Persian. "If we're going to have something different every day, then why can't it be today?"

"Why not *uzum*?" asked the Turk.

"Why not *stafilia*?" demanded the Greek.

"Believe me," said the Persian, "that which I said is the best of all."

The Arab became angry. "Impossible! I won't eat *angur*!"

The Turk insisted, "*Uzum!*"

The Greek rose to his feet too. "Are you trying to make fools of us? Then, what am I doing here anyway?"

And the four beggars began to quarrel in loud voices.

At that moment an old man passing by approached the men and asked what they were arguing about. "Brothers! Why are you arguing? Take it easy and let's see what this is all about."

So they told him the story and finished saying, "We are living together and we each want to eat what we want. We have only this one coin, but one wants *angur*, another *inab*, another *uzum*, and still another *stafilia*! Each one has a different liking."

The old man laughed. "Is that all it is?"

"Yes," they answered, "that's what it's about. It's true that eating or not eating something is not all that important, but the problem is that no one wants to give in to the other, and that's not a laughing matter."

As it happened, the old man knew Persian, Arabic, Turkish, and Greek. He laughed again.

"You are right," he said. "No one wants to be forced. But I am laughing because there is no question of force here. Your dispute is a dispute about words. You are wasting your time arguing. I know that you have no disagreement."

"What does that mean?" asked the four.

"It means," said the old man, "that most wars and disputes are like your disagreement over what to eat. They arise from ignorance and lack of information. All of the people living in this world want the same thing. Big differences are about other things."

"What are you trying to say?"

"I want to know whether each of you is ready to take his portion of the money for himself and with it that of the others?"

"Ah!" they said. "It's nothing like that! It's not a question of more or less. We're arguing about the kind of food."

"Look!" said the old man. "Big disputes are always about more or less, so you don't have a big dispute. Know then that all of you want the same thing! *Angur* and *inab* and *uzum* and *stafilia* are all the same thing! Grapes! Instead of letting your argument grow worse, go and buy some grapes and eat them in happiness."

The four men were delighted and laughed. "O good man, may God prolong your life. We didn't know, and we were about to start fighting with our fists. Now we've learned that we'd better improve our understanding before we take offense."

So they bought the grapes and they ate them together in friendship. They vowed never to forget the lesson of the grapes.

17
THE LANGUAGE OF ANIMALS

One day a man went to Moses and said, "O Moses, I have believed in you for many years, but I haven't gotten any benefit from your religion. So I've come to you today with a request."

"Tell me what your request is," Moses said. "If I can, I'll do it."

"I want you to ask God," said the man, "to teach me the language of animals. I want to learn valuable lessons from their conversations."

"I don't want to be a spoilsport," said Moses, "but I don't think this would be advisable for you. You can learn as much as you need from your own experience and the experiences of your friends, and also from books and the records of the lives of others. Do you think that you have learned everything there is to be learned from those things so that now you must learn from the animals too? First, go and learn as much as you can using your own human language, and that should be enough for seventy generations! As for learning the language of animals, that's just a whim and idle longing. Too much of that brings trouble to a man."

But the man was insistent. "No, I don't want to use the language of animals for personal gain. I want to understand some new things. I have dogs in my house. I have chickens. I have donkeys. I have sheep. I want to know what they're saying to each other. I want to improve my own character through their words."

"Very well," said Moses. "You want to know what they are saying! I want to know many things too, but when it isn't right, it's better not to know. Come, listen to me. Put away this fancy and go back to your work. Don't think too much about being clever, for too much cleverness may bring with it much woe."

But the man said, "I can't give it up. I've got to learn the language of animals. I'll accept the pain and trouble. You are not ungenerous; ask God to teach me the language of chickens and dogs. I'll be satisfy if I learn just those two!"

"Very well," sighed Moses. "As long as you are willing to accept the trouble it may bring, I'll pray that you may understand the language of chickens and dogs. But I'm not responsible if you lose by it."

Happy and pleased, the man went home. When night came, he went to sleep and woke up early the next morning. He said to his servant, "Bring me breakfast, and let the dog and rooster come in."

The servant released the dog from the kennel and the rooster from the chicken coop, then prepared his master's breakfast. When he brought it, a piece of bread fell to the floor from his hand. The rooster jumped up, snatched the bread and ate it. The dog grumbled, saying, "What a rotten rooster you are! You eat wheat. You eat millet. You eat barley. You eat flies. You eat cockroaches. You hunt in the garden and eat earthworms and a thousand other things. You know that I can't get anything other than that bread. Yet you wouldn't even let me eat that one bread crumb!"

"Don't fret," said the rooster. "In its place, tomorrow will be a happy day for you. Meat is tastier than anything else to you, and tomorrow the master's horse will fall dead and you'll be able to eat as much meat as you want."

"Good," said the dog. "I'd forgotten about that. As long as things are thus, you eat the bread. Enjoy your meal!"

Upon hearing this exchange, the master mused, "Incredible! So the horse is going to die tomorrow! It's a good thing that I found this out. Learning the language of animals is indeed useful."

He immediately summoned his groom and said to him, "Take that horse to the market and sell it for whatever it will bring."

The groom took the horse to the market and sold it. He gave the money to his master, who was delighted that he had not lost the value of the horse.

The following morning at breakfast the master threw a piece of bread to the dog. But the rooster was too nimble and snatched the bread from in front of the dog.

Said the dog, "Dear rooster, look, yesterday you said that the horse would die, but it didn't happen. The master sold it. And today once again you are eating the breakfast bread and I must remain hungry until noon."

"I didn't lie," said the rooster. "The horse was supposed to die, but the master sold it, and the horse died in the stable of the man who bought it. But since it was ordained that the master must suffer some loss and it didn't happen yesterday, today his donkey will die. The death of a donkey is like a wedding feast for a dog. Tomorrow you'll eat meat, but I won't as I can't eat meat."

"That's right," exclaimed the dog. "I'd forgotten. May the bread nourish you!"

Having heard this, the master immediately called his groom and told him to take the donkey to the market and sell it for whatever price he could get.

On the third day the dog said to the rooster at breakfast, "You say something every day and your promises make me feel good, but the next day you go back on your word and there is no meat. Forget about the first day, when the master's horse was supposed to die but he sold it instead. The second day when I had hopes of eating donkey meat, he sold the donkey! If that's the way it is to be, you shouldn't eat the bread at breakfast. After all, I have some rights in this household, too!"

"That's right," said the rooster. "But I don't understand how the master has become so smart and astute. Every day he fends off another loss! However, anything which has a substitute is no cause for complaint. This morning at dawn while I was praying, I heard that in place of the horse and donkey which the master has sold, four of his black sheep will die. Well, when they die, the bodies will be taken and thrown away in the desert, as carrion meat is unlawful. Then you can go to the desert and eat as much as you want! It's lawful for you."

"I know about that," said the dog. "One can't prevent all loss. The horse was sold and the donkey was sold. In their place the black sheep will die. Fine. I'll be patient."

Upon hearing this, the master ordered his shepherd to take the four black sheep to the market and sell them.

The shepherd did as he was told, and the master said to himself, "The knowledge of the language of animals is indeed very profitable!"

And he was very pleased with himself:

He thanked God and rejoiced, saying,

"I've prevented loss from my own property;
"After learning the speech of dogs and chickens,
"I've gained gold and sold loss!"

So the next day, when the rooster and the dog got
together for breakfast, the dog quarreled with the rooster,
saying, "It's my turn today! I know what was supposed to
happen, but it all turned out differently. The horse was
sold, the donkey was sold, and even the sheep were sold!
But I can't stay hungry until noon every day. Our master
is very clever. Whatever loss there is supposed to be, he
prevents it!"

"Don't count too much on the master's cleverness,"
replied the roster. "Too much shrewdness can end badly.
For the master himself will die today! Then his family and
relatives will give alms. They'll distribute bread, they'll
distribute stew. They will slaughter sheep. There will be
much to enjoy, and you'll have your portion, too!"

"Oh!" exclaimed the dog. "How do you know that?"

"When I was at prayer this morning," said the rooster,
"I heard it. Our master wasn't supposed to die this soon,
but he has acquired some things unlawfully. Just as when
a person's blood is diseased, his blood is let out by cupping,
or leeches are applied to suck out the bad blood, so he was
supposed to suffer some losses to compensate for this. His
horse was to die, but the clever man sold it. Then in place
of that, the donkey was supposed to die, but the master

sold the donkey too. Then the four sheep were supposed to die, but he prevented any loss to himself from that. These were supposed to compensate for injuries of the unlawful acts to his soul. Since he didn't allow those things to happen, now the calamity will fall on his own neck! He cannot sell that!"

"How strange!" said the dog.

"Yes," continued the rooster, "too much cleverness can be the cause of a disaster, even death!"

Hearing these words, the master trembled with terror. He left his breakfast untouched and hurried to the residence of the prophet. After greeting him, the man said, "O Moses! Help me! I am ruined!"

"What's happened?" asked Moses. "What are you afraid of?"

"It's not just fear," the man said. "I am certain that something awful will happen to me." And then he related what had happened and said, "What can I do? I don't want to die!"

"I warned you that learning the language of animals would bring you no good," said Moses. "There is nothing now that I can do. I can't interfere in God's work. I have no power over life and death. As you said, it had been ordained that you would suffer some property losses, but you prevented them. They were the shield to fend off calamity from you. You wanted to improve your character, but instead you sold your horse, donkey, and sheep and bought trouble for yourself. There can be no cheating in the works of God. I am powerless. . ., but there is one thing you could do. . ."

"I beseech you! Tell me what I should do!"

"Weren't the horse, the donkey, and the sheep supposed

to be alms to protect your life?" asked Moses. "So, you could go to the men who bought the animals and suffered the loss that you were supposed to incur and ask for their forgiveness. Return the money to at least one of them and take the loss upon yourself. If one of them agrees, perhaps your fate will be altered."

"You've spoken rightly," said the man. "I'll go right away and fix things."

He took off running and went to the shepherd. "Whom did you sell the sheep to?" he asked.

"I sold them to Yunus," replied the shepherd.

The master ran to the house of farmer Yunus and said, "Yunus, were you the one who bought four dying black sheep yesterday?"

"Yes," said Yunus. "And it's a good thing that I did! Because all four of them died that very day!"

"No!" said the man. "It was very bad! You suffered a loss, and I've come to make it up to you. I want to return your money to you and I want you to excuse me, because I knew ahead of time that they were going to die when I sold them. I am very sorry for what I did."

"It's not possible for me to take back the money," insisted Yunus. "I'm very happy with the way things turned out. Do you know that I had a dispute with somebody? I wanted to take the four sheep to the judge's house and give them as a bribe so that he would issue a verdict in my favor. But since the sheep died that very day, I wasn't able to do that! Then I heard that the judge had ordered that if anyone brought a bribe to his house, that person would be seized and thrown in prison. The judge said anyone who tries to give a bribe wants to pervert the truth and for that crime he should be punished.

"So, you see, it was a good thing that the sheep died. If they hadn't, I'd be in prison right now. I thank God that a small loss saved me from a greater catastrophe. That's why the purchase was a good deal! The money is yours. I've learned a lesson worth more than a hundred sheep and a thousand pieces of silver."

The man realized that he had failed, so he returned home at once and asked his groom who had bought the donkey.

"Ilyas," the groom answered.

His master rushed to the house of Ilyas and said to him, "Ilyas, did you buy that dying donkey yesterday?"

"Yes, and it's a very good thing that I did, because the donkey died the same day!"

"No," said the master, "that was very bad. You've suffered a loss and I've come now to make it up to you. That donkey was mine and I knew that it was about to die. Now I want to return your money and get your absolution."

"It isn't possible for me to return your money," said Ilyas shaking his head. "I'm very satisfied with the way things turned out. Do you know why I bought that donkey? I bought it because I was very unhappy that I didn't own a donkey. Some of my friends had donkeys and they had decided to ride them to a certain village the night before last. Since I didn't have a donkey, I wouldn't have been able to go with them. I was very upset about that until the day before yesterday, when I bought your donkey in the morning. I told my friends that I would be coming with them after all. But the donkey got sick at noon, fell down, and died. I had to let them know that I wouldn't be able to go with them after all and I was very disappointed.

"My friends left without me and as they were crossing

some open land they met a pack of rabid wolves. The wolves tore their donkeys to pieces and bit them badly. They are still in the hospital. When I heard that, I thanked God that my donkey had died and averted the calamity from my neck. If not, I would now be lying in the hospital, too. If I had bought a different donkey, a healthy one, I would have gone with them and suffered their fate."

Ilyas smiled. "So for this reason I am happy and satisfied with the deal. I don't want your money. Indeed, if you wish, I'll give you more money for that donkey!"

The man saw that he had failed again. He went quickly back to his groom and learned from him who had bought the horse. He sought out the house of Ibrahim and said to him, "Ibrahim, did you buy a horse on the point of death a couple of days ago?"

"Yes, I did, and it's a good thing that I did buy it, because the horse died that very day."

"No," said the man, "that was very bad! That horse was mine and I knew that it was about to die. Now I've come to make restitution and give you your money back so that you will be content with me."

"I can't possibly take the money back," said Ibrahim firmly. "That horse was very beneficial for me and I'm quite satisfied with things the way they are. Do you know that on that day I had to travel on some business to a distant village? I found a traveler going to the same place. He had a horse and I said to myself that I should buy a horse so that I could go with him. I went to the market and bought your horse because it was cheaper than any of the others. A little while later it neighed and fell dead. At first, I was very unhappy about that and I decided not to postpone my trip. Later I learned that that man I was planning to travel with went anyway and fell into the hands of highwaymen in the desert. They took his horse and nearly beat him to death.

"That's why I thanked God that the death of the horse prevented me from going on that journey. Otherwise, I would have lost the horse and God knows what would have happened to me at the hands of those brigands! So I am very satisfied with the loss that saved me from a greater affliction."

"Dear friend," pleaded the man desperately, "now that things are right with you, come and take back your money, because I am sorry that I sold you that dying horse. I'm in deep trouble now that you only can save me from."

"Since you say that you were aware of the horse's defect and you sold the horse deceitfully, I'm not about to do that," replied Ibrahim in a hard voice. "How do I know that there is not another trick in your wanting to give back the money? Whatever it may be, go think of something else. I'm not interested. I am satisfied with the deal that we made and there is no reason to take your money for nothing."

Disappointed once again, the man said to himself, "I'll return to Moses and seek another solution. These people who don't know the language of animals are smarter than I am and should have learned from their actions. I wish that I had not learned the language of animals!"

So the man turned back. On the way he passed his own house. Seeing the rooster sitting on a wall, the man said to him, "Rooster! You have brought all this ruin upon me. I've been feeding you all your life. What business did you have with foretelling the future?"

"I was minding my own business," said the rooster.

"What business did you have with the language of animals when you couldn't learn from the language of people?"

At that moment the man felt sick. He fell to the ground and surrendered his soul to the Creator of Life.

18
THE FALSE FRIEND

Long ago there was a time when the Jews and the Christians were enemies. There was a city in which the Jews outnumbered the Christians and that city had a tyrannical ruler. This ruler saw that his advantage lay in displaying himself as a zealous Jew. The people, too, were oppressing the Christians and every day a number of the Christians were seized and tortured on the pretext of heresy. Nonetheless, the number of Christians increased day by day.

This ruler had an evil vizier who was very shrewd and devious. He was also very zealous and would say that every person must become a Jew and no one should be a Christian.

One day the vizier said to the ruler, "It's not enough just to show open hostility to the Christians as you do. First, the people hide their beliefs and then when the people see your oppression, they become Christians, because people always love the oppressed and despise the oppressor. If we want to eliminate the Christians, we must adopt a better plan and have a strategy."

"For example, what?" asked the ruler.

"I have a good plan," said the vizier. "In order to spread my poison among them and eradicate them, I am ready to sacrifice myself and suffer for a while, but you must implement my plan while keeping it secret."

"The truth is," the ruler said, "I want to be more powerful than anyone else and I want to rule the world! I'll do whatever you say. Now, tell me your plan."

"This is the way to do it," said the vizier. "Order that I be seized and whipped in the public square. My feet will be beaten. Bloody and bruised, I will be dragged to the foot of gallows where you will say, 'Since this vizier has become a Christian and has left the religion of his parents, we must hang him as a warning to others.'

"You will have secretly commanded one of the lords to come forth as an arbitrator at that moment. He will intercede on my behalf and save me from the gallows and you will say, 'Now that things are thus, I will expel this treacherous vizier from the city.' The news will spread throughout the city that the vizier has been thrown out of the city as a warning to others because he has become a Christian.

"Then I shall take refuge in the country of the Christians and cry out: 'What a time and period we live in! No one has the right to choose his own religion. They won't let people worship God as their hearts tell them to.'

"When the Christians are certain that I am a Christian sharing their beliefs, they will come to trust me. Then I shall take care of the rest. I'll create a turmoil among the Christians that will have no end! There is no calamity worse than sedition and disagreement. When they are disputing and fighting among themselves, they'll be weakened. After I've executed my scheme, I'll flee and we will become stronger than all!"

"A good plan!" exclaimed the ruler. "If you can tear out the roots, then the branches and leaves of the Christians will wither in our country too. Good fortune will be mine! But can you do all this by yourself?"

"Destruction," smiled the vizier, "is always easier than construction. I will plant the sapling of enmity among them and light the fire of contention. They will fall upon each other's throats. They will finish the job themselves and I won't be alone."

"Excellent!" said the ruler. "What could be better? May the God of Moses reward you!"

So the next day the ruler commanded that the fanatical Jew be seized because he had left his religion and become a Christian. He was beaten and tied up and brought to the foot of the gallows. Someone came and interceded for his life, as had been arranged. Then he was driven out of the city and everyone said that the vizier had left the religion of his father and mother and become a Christian. "He's become an unbeliever," the people shouted. "Down with the traitorous vizier!"

All this was done. The vizier was beaten and injured and fled to the Christians. As they had already heard about what had happened to him, they greeted him and honored him. The deceitful vizier denounced the Jewish ruler constantly. He even said, "I've been a Christian for years and the ruler finally became aware of it. He drove me out with insults and disgrace. If Lord Jesus had not protected my soul, that Jewish ruler would surely have killed me."

He thanked God profusely that the Christians had given him refuge. The Christians who knew that he had been the Jewish ruler's vizier, said, "This man has gone to the door of death and returned for the beliefs and faith which we have. Now we must honor and respect him."

So the vizier began to attract the people around him and discuss Christianity with them. Since he was widely read and had a lot of knowledge, and was a smooth talker to boot, most of the people gradually became his disciples and would tell others about his marvelous words.

Little by little it came to pass that there was no speaker among the Christians more famous than he. Even the ruler of the Christian country believed in him. The Christian theologians chose him as their leader and gave him the right to issue orders and decrees. They called him the "regent of Jesus."

It was said everywhere that the light of faith shone forth from the forehead of this regent of Jesus and his tongue spoke the truth. He had contact with the heavenly angels and he even met with Jesus himself one night a week in the fourth heaven! Such stories arise among the common people when they become disciples and the people believe them.

During this period when most of the Christians believed that the vizier's speech was revelation form God, the Jewish ruler wrote him a letter in which he said, "Don't forget your agreement and promise."

The vizier rote in reply, "Don't worry. I've finished my preparations and I'll light the fire very soon."

In those days, the Christians were divided into twelve sects and each of them had a leader whom his followers obeyed. These twelve religious leaders were also devoted to the regent of Jesus, because they had come to have great faith in his knowledge, virtue, and abstinence. They obeyed his orders as they would have obeyed the orders of Jesus himself.

Now that the enemy in the guise of a friend had firmly laid the foundations of his plan, he secretly ordered a stonecutter to make twelve stone tablets. The vizier had devised twelve sets of rules of conduct and religious law, none of which agreed with another, and then ordered the stonecutter to inscribe each set upon a stone.

On one was written: "It is the command of God that mankind become monks and leave the world. They must worship night and day and leave the world's work to the worldly while they meditate upon the Last Day."

On another was written: "God has no need of prayer, wailing, and worship. Mankind must eat at the dining cloth of the world and drink and be happy. God created all these blessings for the enjoyment of the people and He will forgive them their sins on the Last Day."

On another was written: "If someone strikes you on one cheek, offer him the other so that he may strike it. God will settle accounts on the Day of Resurrection and the send the wrongdoer to hell. Violence is bad, but the punishment for it is up to God. Enduring threats and violence is virtuous and God will compensate for it."

On still another was written: "Now that human beings have understanding, they must themselves make the laws by which they live according their own desires. God does not interfere in the affairs of mankind. They are fortunate who either by counsel or force cause others to adhere to them. Each person must seize his own rights with his own hands."

In short, the twelve stone tablets were prepared, each with a set commandments contradicting the others. Then he invited the twelve leaders who were rulers in separate sections of the country to come to him one by one. He gave each man one of the tablets secretly so that the others might not know about it and said to him:

"In order that the commandments of God may be implemented exactly, I have had them inscribed upon this stone so that no one will be able to alter them. Since you are the greatest among the twelve leaders and the most beloved, I am entrusting it to you so that you can guide the people along the right and true path. Do not show this stone to anyone except the most trustworthy of your sect."

So the twelve leaders departed and each one adopted a set of rules according to the commandments on the stone he had received. He taught them as God's law to his disciples. Things reached a point in which the followers of each of the twelve leaders began to consider the others heretics and sinners.

And thus the seeds of dispute and public turmoil were sown among them.

Whenever there was a disagreement, the leaders would come to the regent of Jesus and seek his counsel. He would calm them with excuses and say, "Only God knows what is right for the people. Every person must act according to commandments which have been given to him. Of course, some will be lost and some will make mistakes, but little by little they will become more knowing and be corrected."

Day by day, the signs of public unrest became more apparent. Then the regent of Jesus employed another trick. He closed the hall in which he preached and locked the doors of his house to outsiders, saying, "I've received a command from God not to speak with anyone and that no one should see me. Anyone who has a problem should take

it to his own religious leader and get the decision from
him."

On that very day, he once again summoned the twelve
religious leaders one by one and took each one aside
secretly and said to him: "I must travel to heaven. So that
Christianity may remain on earth, I must appoint one of
you twelve leaders as my deputy. And that one person is
you! Go and guide the people in accordance with the commandments written upon the stone which you have
received. All of the other leaders must follow your orders.
Anyone who disagrees with you is a heretic and you have
the right to use any means to bring him back to the true
faith, whether it be peacefully or by force."

He said this to one, then another, then the third, the
fourth, the fifth, and so on until he had told each of the
twelve the same thing. Then he sent them back separate-
ly to their own regions, saying, "Tonight I shall ascend to
Heaven and my spirit will be watching and witnessing
what you do on earth."

Having said this, that very night he abandoned his
house and establishment and fled the country. But the
people supposed that the regent of Jesus had indeed
ascended to heaven!

So the Jewish vizier, after having sown the seeds of
conflict, returned to the Jewish ruler and said, "Now, I've
planted the seeds that will bear fruit for many years to
come. There is no longer any need for your force and your
being blamed. The Christians will destroy themselves by
themselves, because quarreling and partisanship will ruin
a people more completely than anything else."

And so it happened that afterwards each of the twelve
Christian leaders thought himself the only true leader and

would not accept the others as equals. Since their sets of
commandments differed, one from another, every day dis-
agreements arose between the groups of followers. Each
leader considered himself in the right and the others in
the wrong. Fighting and brawling erupted among the
Christians. There were daily battles among the sects.
Thus, peace and tranquillity were lost among them.

This was the state of affairs until one of the Christians
who was serving in the court of the Jewish ruler and had
kept his religion secret learned of the secret plan. He
informed the Christian ruler who in turn summoned the
great men and elders and the twelve religious leaders to
his court. When they had assembled, he said to them, "God
is one and the law of God should be one, too. You who are
squabbling among yourselves must show the proofs and
sources of your ideas."

One by one, the leaders of the twelve sects said, "We
have an inscribed stone. It's secret and no one else may
look at it."

Said the ruler, "Nobody can accept such a thing!
Anything taught in secret is heresy. The truth is that
which even an opponent can consider and weigh in his
mind. People have heads and can recognize the truth. We
must compare these stone tablets with each other. If they
are in agreement, we must investigate other sources for
the differences among you. If they are not, then we must
find a solution. No prophet has ever had a secret book or
law or commandment. Only bad things are concealed.
Whatever is good should be in the open."

So they had to produce the stone tablets and compare
them. Everyone saw that the regent of Jesus had been an
enemy trickster in the guise of a friend. As they all agreed

that the law of God must be the same for all mankind, when they saw the differences among the commandments, the scales fell from their eyes. They made peace with each other and the disputes vanished.

During this time, news arrived that both the Jewish ruler and his fanatical vizier had been removed from power. A more just Jewish king was on the throne. The Christian ruler and the new Jewish ruler exchanged letters and they agreed not to be enemies. They invited their peoples to peace and happiness and proclaimed in writing:

"To Jesus his religion and to Moses his religion.

"No one has the right to impose his beliefs on others by force. Religion is for the comfort of mankind, not for their oppression. Religion is for building, not for tearing down. Whoever creates destruction and differences among people is a sinner before God. So long as a person does not trouble others, his beliefs are to be respected."

Many copies of this proclamation were made and the leaders of both religions sealed and signed them. They posted them on the walls of every city. And the people busied themselves with their work and their lives in peace and cooperation.

19
THE TWO SLAVES

In those days when male and female slaves were bought and sold, a rich man ordered his steward to buy two young male slaves from the slave market. So the two were bought, one for one hundred dirhams, and the other for twenty.

When the slaves were brought to their new master's house, he summoned one of them. He was a handsome, fair youth. Upon entering he greeted his master and stood respectfully with his hand on his breast. His master him his name.

"Jamal," he replied, which means 'handsomeness.'

"Bravo, what a beautiful name you have!" exclaimed his master. "You yourself are indeed very handsome."

He asked about some other things and found the young man intelligent, well-spoken, and polite. Whatever he was asked, he answered promptly and courteously. The master was very pleased with his purchase and commented, "You were bought for one hundred dirhams, but you are worth a thousand!"

After that he called for the other slave. This one was not handsome and had no apparent qualities. He was a dark, short, downcast, and dejected youth. He saluted his owner and sat on a stool in front of him.

"What is your name?" asked the master.

"Ka-mal." he answered.

"There is no such name as Ka-mal," said the master,

Jamal began to laugh at the other slave's pronuncia-
tion. "He means to say that his name is Kamal, but his
accent is like that."

"All right," said the master. He posed a few more questions to Kamal and listened to his answers. He saw that
Kamal was also intelligent and not without common
sense. Then he sent Jamal out and said to Kamal, "It's
obvious that you have a sound mind, but your teeth are in
bad condition and you have bad breath. Sit back a little
and don't talk too much until I can send you to a physician
for treatment."

After that, the master had Jamal sent to the bath so
that the young man could wash off the dirt of travel. The
master then remained alone with the second slave so that
he could test his character and bearing some more.

"I've heard that you two worked together in the same
house. So, tell me, Kamal, why you were sold?"

Said Kamal, "I don't know. One day the master ordered
us to be sold. Perhaps he had found some better servants.
Or perhaps he didn't have enough work for us. People
don't tell us their secrets. They don't trust us because we
are slaves. Anyway, it doesn't make any difference to us."

"Were you living conditions there good?" the master
asked. "Were you pleased with your master?"

"Pleased?" said the slave. "What can I say? So long as
a man isn't free, he is not content. But, anyway, we were
living as everyone lives. We worked, we ate our bread, and
passed time. Our master himself was not idle. We all

worked."

"Tell me," said the master, "is what Jamal said about you true?"

Kamal looked at his master in surprise, but said, "I don't believe that my fellow worker would lie about me, because I've never done him any wrong. Whatever he said is certainly true."

"But," continued the master, "in my opinion you are a very valuable young man. From the very beginning I knew that you were trustworthy, but he said that you were very envious. He said that you were disloyal. He said that you were nosy and an informer. That's what he said."

"If Jamal said such things," shrugged Kamal, "then they must be true. I don't know about being envious, but I do hope to make progress in life. I think about people who are more popular liked than I am. Perhaps that could be called envy. I don't know about being disloyal, but if someone wants me to help him betray our employer, I won't cooperate with him. Perhaps that is called disloyalty.

"I don't know about being nosy and an informer, but if someone sends me on an errand, I do it as thoroughly as possible. I learn as much as I can and then bring the information back. I also give my own opinion. Perhaps that should be called nosiness and informing. And it's possible that Jamal didn't lie. No one knows his own deficiencies and I don't either. Perhaps that was what Jamal meant."

"Now," said the master, "so that I can trust you and speak openly with you, I want you to tell me about every fault that you have noticed in Jamal. That way I'll know how to deal with him."

"I haven't noticed any faults in him," said Kamal. "Jamal is a cheerful and polite young man. In every place he is better regarded than I am. His price is one hundred dirhams, and mine is twenty. I think he has good qualities that all can see and for that reason his value is several times mine. Good and bad can never be concealed."

"Very well," said the master. "Now that you have come here, are you happy here. Do you think this place is better than your last, or not?"

"My duty is to work and serve," Kamal said. "It doesn't make any difference where I work. Because I am a slave and in bondage and I'm not free, I can never be happy. But that is God's command and my fate. I've just arrived here today and I don't know whether this place is better or not. With the passage of time, I'll get to know you better and you'll get to know me better. I don't know what else to say now. I always try to do the work given me and do it well."

In his heart the master praised Kamal's decency and honesty. At that moment, Jamal returned from the bath. The master sent Kamal with an old man to the doctor and then began to test Jamal some more. He began asking the same questions.

"I've heard, said the master, "that the two of you worked in the same house. So, why were you sold?"

"It wasn't my fault," answered Jamal. Kamal was so lazy and talked back so much that the owner took to disliking me too because I was with him. He said that since we were living together, he would sell us together. But I think he may have found some other slaves better than we were."

"How were you living conditions there," enquired the master. "Were you happy with your master?"

"No, sir! What kind of a life did we have? We worked like dogs and still he found fault with us! A couple times

Kamal said that we should steal his money and run away, but I told him that would be wrong. Anyway, the master's unfairness did its work and he sold us and good riddance!"

"Tell me, is what your fellow worker Kamal says about you true?"

"No, sir! Kamal is so wicked that he's always saying bad things about me. You can see from his appearance that he's no good. With that black color and that awkward physique how dare he find fault with me! It's good that he doesn't look like a human being. His outside tells you what his heart is like. You can never believe anything that ugly black says!"

"Well," said the master, "in my opinion you are a fortunate young man. From the very first I understood that you were not a bad person, but Kamal said that you're very envious. He said that you were very disloyal. He said that you were nosy and an informer. He said all those things."

"Look, sir," said Jamal, "when I say that Kamal is malicious, you can know from that. It's Kamal who can't stand to see me better off than himself. His envy has made him black. It is Kamal, too, who is disloyal and slanders me at that every opportunity. Kamal is the nosy parker and tattler who will come to you bearing tales and to lie about me. In fact, if I told you everything about him that I know, you would wouldn't keep him for an hour! Instead you'd sell him off for half his price! The thieving brat has no shame! How dare he say such things about me?"

"Good!" said the master. "Now, so that I can trust you and speak frankly with you, I want you to tell me all of Kamal's faults that you have observed so that I may decide how I should deal with him."

"What can I say?" said Jamal. "If you want to hear my

opinion, Kamal is nothing but trouble. He can't speak properly and doesn't even know his own name! He says 'Ka-mal.' He doesn't know how to do anything except talk back and complain about everything! Tomorrow, if you send him on an errand, he will tell everyone he meets that his master is this way and that way! Black and ugly; the only part of him that works is his tongue!"

"Let's move on," said the master. "Tell me, now that you have come here, are you happy? Do you think this place is better than your last place or not?"

"What a question, sir!" exclaimed Jamal. "Of course I am happy! There is no comparison between you and my former master. You are a perfect lord and superior to all others. I used to see your image in my dreams, and now that I've come here, all of my hopes and dreams have been fulfilled! Oh! How I was suffering at the hands of my former master! I know that this place will be very much better."

"Very good," said the master. "I know everything I need to know. Now, go outside and wait until Kamal comes back and I will give you my instructions."

After Kamal had returned, the master called them both to him and said, "I've examined both of you. Kamal, you have no fault except that your living conditions were not good and you fell sick causing you to have bad breath. I shall have you treated and you will always stay with me.

"But you, Jamal, you have become conceited because of your outer appearance and you think that everyone is like yourself, superficial. There is an old saying: The external beauty is nothing, O brother! Bring me the beauty of character!"

The master continued:

"Because Kamal has good intentions and would not be unfair about his fellow worker even in his absence, I trust him. From this moment on, you, Jamal, must work under his supervision. Instead of manners and flattery, learn diligence and cooperation from Kamal. Then we shall see what happens. You must obey everything Kamal says."

Behind the master's house there was a garden. It was Kamal and Jamal's job to dig a channel in it for irrigation. From the very first day, Jamal sat down after an hour or so and said, "I'm tired. I can't do this kind of work! We certainly have fallen into the hands of a cruel master. Why don't we do the work poorly so that he will get exasperated and sell us? We might get a better master next time."

"No, dear Jamal," Kamal said. "Don't be unhappy. I'll work harder and make up what you can't do. The master won't find out. Be patient and everything will turn out all right. How do we know we won't get a worse master?"

"Yes," said Jamal. "You say that now, but when you were alone you said so many bad things about me that he put you in charge."

"No, dear friend," said Kamal. "Don't think that. If you want to know what I said, I'm ready to repeat everything the master and I said."

So Kamal related the master's questions and his own answers. Then he said, "Now you tell me what you said about me."

When Jamal realized that the master had said exactly the same thing to both of them, he said, "I can't tell you. When the master told me that you had said bad things about me, I believed him. I tried to make myself appear in a better light to him. Now I know that what he was saying was a test, and I failed the test and now you are taking on yourself my burden. For this reason I confess that you have a right to superiority over me."

Things remain thus until the master decided to go on a journey. Since he had not forgotten the two slaves, he sold Jamal for two hundred dirhams, but he couldn't find a buyer for Kamal. So the master set him free for the pleasure of God. Then he adopted him as his son, and they went on the trip together, like a father and a son.

20
ELEPHANTOLOGY IN THE DARK

Several Indians used to travel from India with an elephant. They would put it on exhibition in countries where the people had never seen an elephant and collect money. In this way they supported themselves.

One evening the Indians entered a city and took up residence in a house. People who had seen the elephant on the way and heard about the owners of the elephant spread the news that the Indians had arrived with their elephant and were in a such-and-such a house and intended to exhibit the animal to the public.

Most of the people thought, "Fine. When they put the Indian elephant on display we'll go to look at it."

But there were some who had no patience to wait to view the strange animal. They were in a hurry to see the it before the others. Then, wherever they went, they could brag, "Yes, we saw the elephant before everyone else. An elephant is thus and so."

By doing this they would be able to establish their superiority and importance over others. So, as soon as they heard about the arrival of the elephant, these persons gathered at the door of the Indians' house and demanded to see the elephant that very night!

"We've just arrived after a long trip," said the owners of the elephant. "We're tired. We haven't gotten the exhibition of the elephant ready yet. It would be better if you came back tomorrow."

"No," insisted the impatient men. "We won't leave until we see the elephant! We are supports of elephants and elephant culture. We absolutely must see the elephant this very night."

"Please," said the Indians. "It isn't possible. There's no light in the elephant's stable."

Replied the eager men, "That doesn't matter. We can examine it even in the darkness. We won't be able to sleep if we don't get to see the elephant tonight! We have to see it before anyone else."

"Very well," said the Indians. "If you are in such a hurry, the ticket on the opening night costs twice as much as on other days."

"No problem! We'll pay three times as much!"

The Indians then said, "You'll have no more than one minute to look at it."

"We agree! Even one minute is worth the trouble. If you want to beat us, we'll let you! We want the elephant! The elephant or death!"

There was nothing for the Indians to do but collect the money and guide the impatient elephantologists to the stable. Most of them went in to see the elephant, but one of their number stayed back and didn't enter the stable.

"Why don't you go in?" asked the Indians.

"I've read in a book," the man said, "that the elephant is a large animal. I too would like to visit the elephant before the others, but I can't see in the dark. Please, you who know elephants better than anyone else, be my teacher for a moment and describe it."

One of the Indians said, "Congratulations! It appears that you are a man of understanding! The way to learn is like this: first you ask for information from people who know more than you do. You read books and learn what others have learned and understood. You research more and in that way understand more."

The elephant keeper continued to explain: "The elephant is an animal like a horse or a camel, but much bigger and heavier. The difference between an elephant and a horse and a camel is that the elephant doesn't have a neck. Its head is stuck right on its body. It's mouth is under its face. Since it doesn't have a neck to stretch to the ground to eat plants, it has a trunk instead. The trunk is like a long leather pipe and is in place of a nose. An elephant drinks water with its trunk and brings grass and vegetation to its mouth with it. The elephant also has two long teeth that can be a yard long. They are its ivory tusks and their value equals that of the elephant itself.

"Moreover, an elephant is very strong and very good for riding. They put a litter (*howdah*) on its back that can carry several people. The elephant is mostly found in hot countries. . ."

While they were talking the one minute was up and the spectators came out of the stable.

The impatient men had gone to the room in which the elephant was kept. As it had been pitch dark, they had approached the animal by groping and feeling. When they reached the elephant, they had the honor of looking at it by means of touching its body. Since they hadn't seen the shape of the animal, each one formed a different opinion about the animal's appearance.

One felt the trunk, another a tusk. Still another touched the flank of the elephant, another the leg. Another felt the tail. In any event, when they came out of the stable, they were all very happy.

They went together from that place until they came upon a street where there was a crowd of guests coming out from a wedding celebration. Each one of the elephantologists found some friends and acquaintances among the guests and began to brag about the accomplishment of having seen the elephant before everyone else. They were eager to show off their personal knowledge of the animal.

"Yes, the Indians brought the elephant. They were going to put it on exhibit in a few days, but we went to see the animal this very night."

The people exclaimed, "How wonderful! This very night? Good, what was the elephant like?"

Then each one of the elephantologists described the animal as he understood it to be.

The man who had felt the trunk said, "An elephant really is odd! It's a long animal like a snake that hangs on a tree. It bends, it straightens out. It makes a loop. It becomes like a pipe. It uncoils. In short, it's very frightening! As soon as I saw it, I got scared and stood aside."

The man who had felt the legs of the elephant said, "The elephant it is not as remarkable as people say. It's like two columns that meet at the top. Like two strong and heavy pillars, but it is continually raising and lowering its feet. If it steps on you, you'd be crushed."

The men who had felt the belly and back of the elephant and investigated it more, said that the elephant was like a throne that had four legs. It has a big roof on which it carries people.

Those who had felt the tusks and tail of the elephant said other things. Listening to all these things, the people from the wedding were sorry that they hadn't been able to see the elephant themselves.

But when the man who had not gone into the stable heard these stories, he wasn't able to control himself.

"Nothing of what they are saying is correct," he cried. "I know what an elephant is better than they do."

The people raised their heads and asked, "Have you seen the elephant too?"

"I haven't seen it," he said, "but I was with my friends. I'd read in a book that the elephant is a huge beast, but I'd never seen its picture. So, when they went in to visit the elephant in the darkness, I asked the elephant keepers about it." Here he described the elephant as its keepers had done. "It's plain that my friends have each only learned about a part of the whole."

The impatient elephant-lovers did not say another word! When the day came that the elephant was displayed and everyone flocked to see it, only those who had heard what the reader of books had said were not surprised at its appearance. Even his friends who had been so quick to form an opinion about the animal now laughed at their own words. They realized that that was about as much as one could learn by studying an elephant in the dark!

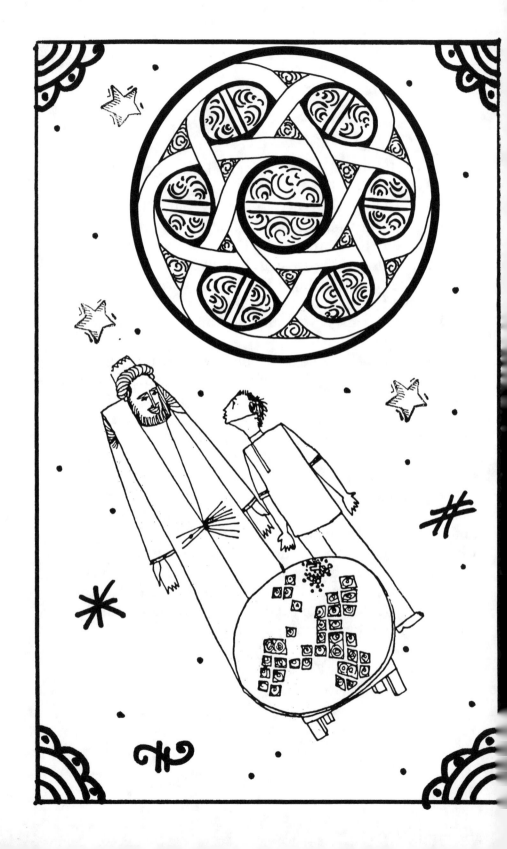

21
THE BOY SWEETSELLER

Once there was a man named Shaykh Ahmad Khidhri who was well-known in his own city for goodness and charity. In his own time, Shaykh Ahmad was a rich, prosperous man, but gradually he gave away his wealth to the poor and the indigent until had had nothing left for himself. The people, however, had gotten used to his generosity and continued to seek his aid. Whenever a stranger came to their town and had no place to stay, he would be directed to Shaykh Ahmad's house. Whenever someone was in debt or was in some financial difficulty, he would head for the shaykh's home.

The good shaykh took delight in helping the needy, so if some deserving person applied to him, he wasn't able to say no to him. As he had nothing of his own left to give, he would go to his friends and neighbors and borrow money in order to help the needy out of their troubles.

Sometimes his family would complain, "We'll never be able to repay the money we have borrowed."

The shaykh would reply, "I'm not doing this for myself. I'm doing this in the Way of God. God will provide. So far we've managed. As for the future, well, God is great!"

By and by, the shaykh's debts reached seven hundred dinars, and in those days seven hundred dinars was a lot of money. But people who lent him money saw that he gave all that he borrowed to the needy, so they didn't press him.

"Shaykh Ahmad is a good man," they would say. "If he weren't able to pay us back eventually, he wouldn't be borrowing from us. He probably has some big expectations and that is why he borrows money now."

It also occasionally happened that people who had faith in the shaykh and his charities, gave him small sums of money for the fulfillment of vows. The shaykh was able to take care of the small personal expenses of his household with this money. Still, whenever there was a problem and someone came to him for help, he was unable to refuse. So he would borrow some more money. Little by little, the townsfolk began to refer to him as 'the debtor shaykh.'

And so things remained until one day, the good shaykh fell ill. His illness became more serious. People began to say that the shaykh didn't have much longer to live and that he was about to kick the bucket!

Shaykh Ahmad's creditors began to worry. "That man has been living by borrowing money for years," they said to each other. "If he dies, none of us will get his money back. There is nothing to do but to ask for our money while he is still alive."

So the creditors arranged to go to the shaykh together. "O shaykh," they said, "we have been lending you money when you needed it for many years, but you have never thought about paying us back. We can't wait any longer. If you don't have the means to repay us, you've been doing us an injustice. Winning friends and buying a good name for yourself with other folks' property is not fair. If you have the money, settle our accounts now!"

"You are right," sighed the shaykh. "You've been patient until now, please be patient a little while longer. It isn't my intention to cause anyone loss. I'm waiting for some money that is sure to arrive soon."

"No person wishes to cause another loss of property," said the creditors, "but when someone has large debts and can't repay, what is there to do? You see, we also have obligations. We didn't find our money in the river or in a rubbish heap! If we had squandered our property senselessly in gifts and donations, we wouldn't have had anything to lend you. You don't understand finance. You take money with one hand and give it away with the other! It's true that you are doing charity, but charity should be given by those who have something to give. Now, we all respect you. Since you are a good man we don't want to bring shame upon you, but what is to be done?"

"All right," said the shaykh, "tell me what I should do."

"What you should do? Settle our accounts, or at least set a date for doing so."

"I have no idea about dates," said the shaykh slowly. "All of that is in the hands of God. I am deeply worried about you. Be patient and everything will be all right. I've earned my good reputation over a lifetime and you have no right to defame me in a day! I have expectations in a certain place. I'll try to pay you back as soon as possible. It isn't difficult for God to send me the seven hundred dinars."

"We don't know about that," said the creditors. "Whether God sends it or a human, it doesn't matter to us. Very well, you have expectations from some place. Give us the date! We shall stay right here until you figure it out and set the date to repay us! You have guests every day, so today we shall be your guests!"

"I am honored to have you as guests," said the shaykh. "If you wish to stay, do so. I'll think about the matter, but the hope that I have doesn't have a definite date. Yet maybe it is near."

At this moment a boy carrying sweetmeats in a tray on his head for sale passed by in the lane crying out:

> "Come, I have sweets and sweetmeats,
> I have excellent sweets;
> Nourishing sweets.
> You won't know how good until you eat some!
> Sweets! Here are sweets!
> Very delicious sweets!"

The good shaykh heard the cries of the sweetseller and said to himself, "Whatever will happen, let it happen. A tray of sweets isn't going to add much to a debt of seven hundred dinars! Let my forty-nine be fifty! Since I'm already under the water, let me sink the depth of another straw! Now that I have guests, let it not be said that Shaykh Ahmad is a person to allow his guests go hungry in his house."

He called a servant and said, "Buy that tray of sweets from the boy and bring them here for my guests."

The servant knew that the shaykh didn't have any money to pay for the sweets, but he had learned well, and did not contradict his master. He went outside and called the sweet seller.

"Look, boy, how much is the tray of sweets wholesale?"

"One dinar and thirty dirhams," answered the boy.

The servant shook his head. "That's too much," he said. "We are poor folk and don't have that much money. Guests have arrived unexpectedly, so if you can, sell them for one dinar."

"You don't have much money and you have guests," considered the boy. "All right, I'll do something. My master wants a dinar from me for this tray of sweets. Anyway, I'm, tired. I'll sell you them all to you for one dinar. Where do you want me to take them?"

"Right here, to the house of the shaykh," said the servant

With a smile, the boy brought in the tray of sweets and set them down on the floor of the shaykh's reception hall.

"Sweeten your mouths with these while I think about our problem," said the shaykh to his guests.

So the guests busied themselves with eating the sweets while the shaykh spread his prayer rug in a corner and performed his prayers. After finishing, he confided to God: "O God, Do you see? I spent that seven hundred dinars for You and Your deserving people. This is the last time I shall borrow. Do not shame me in front of this sweetseller. I don't know now what I shall say to him. These people here are the guests of Shaykh Ahmad. Shaykh Ahmad is Your guest."

By the time the shaykh had finished his prayers, the guests had finished off the sweets.

"Now," said the young sweetseller," give me my money so that I may leave."

"Good lad," said the shaykh softly, "I can't pay you just now. I owe money to all of the men you see sitting here. They want their money and you, too, must be patient until the money arrives from some place."

The boy said, "I don't understand such things! I can't wait! You've bought the sweets and now you must give me my money! If I go back late, my boss will want to know why. If I don't bring the money, he'll want to know why. My bill is separate from theirs."

"Your bill is indeed separate from theirs, but not from mine. I owe seven hundred dinars and I don't have a penny. God knows that I have nothing! There is nothing to do but wait."

"What a mess I've fallen into!" cried the boy. "What does 'be patient' mean? Don't make me call a policeman! If you didn't have any money, it wasn't right for you to buy the sweets! People who have their own money eat sweets or they have some one above them who can pay."

The shaykh became very troubled upon hearing these words and his eyes filled with tears.

"You speak the truth, my boy," he said. "Sweets are eaten by people who have money or have some one above them to give the money. I have someone above me and I'm waiting for Him to pay my debtors, because I spent all my own money and the money I borrowed counting on Him."

"Well," said the boy, "that's no reason to cry. Where is that person you are talking about? Is he dead? Is he alive? Lord! Tell him to give the money."

"He is right here," said the shaykh. "He can pay the debts of all debtors."

Then the shaykh's condition suddenly changed and he began to weep loudly.

The boy felt sorry for the shaykh, but he didn't understand his words. Fearing his the anger of his employer, he worry about the money for the sweets increased. He, too, began to cry. While he was crying he said in a loud voice: "I don't know anything! All I want is the money for the sweets! If you didn't have any money, you shouldn't have eaten the sweets! You're being ridiculous! You're pretending to be a dervish! O God, I want my money! I don't understand any of this! Give me my money and I'll be on my way!"

Hearing the loud cries and weeping of the boy sweetseller, neighbors and strangers gathered in the shaykh's house, each one trying to find out what was going on. Why is the shaykh was weeping and the boy causing a commotion with his shouts and cries?

After learning what the situation really was, a newcomer said, "The boy is right. What does it matter to him if the shaykh owes money to others or not?"

Another said, "The fact is that if you don't have any money you shouldn't eat sweets."

Others offered similar comments.

At this juncture, an old man with a canvas bag entered the house and placed the bag together with a letter in front of the weeping shaykh.

"This bag is yours," said the old man. "The letter they wrote is for you too."

Wiping his eyes, the shaykh took the letter and read it aloud:

"The Honorable Shaykh Ahmad Khidhri, Esquire,

"Please accept my salam and greetings. I live in this district. Some years ago, one of your disciples entrusted me with this sealed bag and instructed me, saying, 'Whenever you see that the Shaykh is in great need or difficulty, send this bag of money to him.'

"I was passing by your house today and heard the boy who sells sweets crying for his one dinar. I thought to myself that if you were in need of a single dinar, surely that day of need is today.

So, I am now executing the will of my friend. I entrust this money to you to do with as you wish. I don't want anyone to know who I am. God keep you."

"In the name of God, the Merciful, the Compassionate," said the shaykh. "The day of settling our accounts has now been made known to us!"

He opened the bag and called the boy to him. "Come, lad. You were very impatient, but you were less so than the others. You did well, for you delivered my cry to my superior. Didn't I tell you that there is someone greater above me? Come, take this dinar for the sweets, and take another for yourself. You have delivered me from a great sorrow. Without your cries, my affairs would not have been straightened out."

As Mawlawi says:

> "Without the tearful cries of the boy sweetseller,
> The pot of mercy would not boil!"

They let the boy go home and then counted out the money in the bag. It was exactly seven hundred dinars and Shaykh Ahmad was able to pay back all that he had borrowed.

When the creditors saw the money, they said, "Respected Shaykh, the repayment is not so late and we cannot wait longer if you wish. If you have more pressing expenses, first take care of those."

"No," answered the shaykh shaking his head. "There is

no obligation more necessary than the repayment of debts. Don't stand on ceremony! Take your money and pray for the lad's life. Without him, there would be no money spread out here. It was his weeping that unlocked God's mercy. I wanted only thing from God, I had only one wish. That was to repay the money I owed. God always answers the righteous prayer."

22

SALMAN THE DEAF AND SHABAN THE DEAF

Tanere was an old grocer by the name of Salman who was very hard of hearing, so the people called him 'Salman the Deaf.' Anyone who wanted to buy something from his grocery had to shout to make himself heard. Salman knew that he was deaf, so when he wasn't able to make out what was being said to him, he would say: "I'm hard of hearing. Please speak more loudly."

One day a man named Shaban who lived near the store and who did not pay his bills promptly tried to buy some things on credit. Salman said, "I'm illiterate and I don't keep an account book or a ledger and I don't give credit."

At that moment Shaban conceived a grudge against Salman and was filled with a desire for revenge. He began to make fun of Salman.

Every day Shaban would take a group of his friends and go to Salman's shop. He would get one of his comrades to speak very softly to Salman. Salman, of course, couldn't hear him and he would ask, "Yes, sir. What did you say?"

Shaban's friend would continue to move his lips and

speak softly. Since Salman couldn't hear, he would ask again, "Speak louder. What do you want?"

Then Shaban would come forward and shout in a loud voice, "Uncle, are you deaf? Our friend wants some plane-tree greens."

All of Shaban's friends would then laugh.

Salman, however, would get upset. "I don't have any plane tree greens. This is a grocery store, not a vegetable stand."

That would cause them all to laugh again, and then they would depart.

On another day another of Shaban's friends would go to Salman and repeat the buffoonery. Salman wouldn't be able to hear and Shaban would come forward and say, "Uncle, are you deaf? Our friend wants two yards of canvas."

Shaban's friends would roar with laughter and the grocer would become flustered and answer, "But we don't have cloth. This is a grocery store, not a cloth store."

The grocer was very annoyed at this nonsense. One day he saw Shaban by himself and said to him, "Look, Shaban, I know that I'm deaf, so stop doing what you have been doing! It's very annoying and it won't please God. If you're trying to harass me to get some protection money out of me, I'm telling you plainly I won't pay it! My deafness is a kind of sickness. It's a physical defect, not a sin, and I'm not responsible for it. You aren't making a fool of me. You're just showing others that you are rude and troublesome. An illness is something that can befall anyone. Once I was young like you and in good health. Now I've become old and deaf. You never know what calamity may afflict you tomorrow. So stop doing that and don't bother me anymore."

Said Shaban, "Tell me, will you give me credit?"

"No," said Salman. "I don't give credit to such as you. You're a scoundrel and can't be counted upon. If you were a good man, you wouldn't mock an old man. It isn't right!"

"When they said you're deaf, they were right!" laughed Shaban.

"Very good," said Salman. "I hope that some day you will understand my pain."

So Salman cursed Shaban and that was that. It happened that one day Shaban found that he had become hard of hearing. Perhaps it wasn't because of Salman's curse because the affairs of the world are not often connected with prayers and curses. In any event, Shaban became deaf and could hear what people were saying only with the greatest difficulty.

One day, while conversing with someone, he misunderstood what that person was saying. The man laughed and said to Shaban, "Uncle, are you deaf?"

Shaban became very unhappy at these words and tried to listen very carefully when he was talking with people so as to understand correctly. But it was no use. Gradually he became virtually stone deaf.

Yes, it happens that people go blind, deaf, or lame. All of these conditions are physical defects, but they are not shameful or a sign of sin. But Shaban had been very proud and now he didn't want anyone to know that he was deaf. Whenever he was in conversation, he would concentrate as much as possible to foresee questions and answers and to read the movements of the lips so that his responses would not be inappropriate.

But all these efforts were in vain! In some situations

Shaban became so embarrassed that he regretted conceal-
ing his deafness. One such incident occurred when he
went to a mill.

The mill in his neighborhood was a water mill that had
been built at a distance from a spring. The water from the
spring would enter the flue of the mill and turn the water-
wheel which would in turn drive the millstone. After per-
forming that task, the water would flow under the mill
and into the fields to be used by the farmers for irrigation.
Sometimes the water from the spring would be cut off
above the mill and the mill wouldn't work. Other times the
flow increased and the millstone spun rapidly. The farmers who wanted their wheat, barley, millet, and corn
ground into flour would bring it to the mill. They would
pay the millers a portion of that flour and take the rest
home.

So, on that day Shaban put a load of wheat on a donkey and went to the mill. After unloading the wheat, he
tethered the animal in the lane. The millers ground the
wheat into flour and put it in sacks. Shaban returned and
put the sacks on the donkey and started to go back home.

As soon as he stepped out of the mill, Shaban saw a villager who had a loaded donkey standing at the foot of the
lane. The villager had a load of potatoes he was delivering
to someone, but he hadn't been able to find the house.
When he saw Shaban from a distance, he ran to him to ask
him for directions to that house.

When Shaban saw the man coming towards him, he
started to think. "Well, that man probably wants to go to
the mill and doesn't know the way and he's coming to ask
directions. I'll say, 'Yes, it's right here.' He'll ask, 'Is the
mill working today?' and I'll reply, 'Yes, today is one of

those days.' Then maybe he'll say, 'Then there's a lot of water.' I've already seen the level of the water. It's up to my waist in the channel, so I'll say, 'Yes, up to here,' and point to my waist. Then he'll ask, 'Does this mill grind the wheat into good flour?' And I'll answer, 'Yes, it's excellent.'

At the moment the man reach him, Shaban was still rehearsing these questions and answers. "Peace be upon you," said the villager.

Shaban had been so busy with his plan to conceal his deafness, that he had completely forgotten about the courtesy of replying to a greeting, said, "Yes, it's right here."

"Where's the reply to my greeting?" demanded the villager. "I haven't asked anything yet! What's right here? Are you crazy?"

"Yes," answered Shaban. "Today is one of those days."

"Why are you talking nonsense?" asked the villager with growing annoyance. "Why, were you made to go under mud?"

"Yes," agreed Shaban. "Up to here."

He pointed to his waist.

The villager grew angry. "No, higher! With your manners, it'd be better if they loaded you up like a donkey!"

Shaban thought that the villager had asked him if he had brought wheat to the mill. He said, "One donkey-load."

"That's really the way it should be!" snapped the villager.

"It's excellent," said Shaban with a smile.

The villager thought that Shaban was ridiculing him. He raised his hand threateningly and used it to express his anger at Shaban's crazy behavior.

"Ah!" cried Shaban. "Why are you going to hit me? I

didn't say anything bad."

"Look," said the villager. "If you'd receive some kicks and blows, maybe you'd understand what you are saying! It's too bad that I have work to do. I don't have the patience to bother with you anymore."

The villager tugged at the bridle of his donkey and went off to find someone else to ask about the house he was looking for.

Then Shaban said to himself, "What a strange person! After I had given him the information, he wanted to me up!"

Then he got his donkey and took the flour home.

A while later, he said to himself, "I've heard that local butcher has been ill and bedridden for several days. It'd be a good thing if I went to see how he is today. Visiting the sick has religious merit and I do business with the butcher just about every day. It wouldn't be right not to enquire after him."

So Shaban changed his clothes and went to visit the sick man. On the way he thought carefully. "A visit to the sick isn't lengthy and involved. When I arrive I'll give him my greetings of peace (salam) and he'll reply. Then I'll ask him about his diet and his medication. He'll say soup or peanut broth or something else. I'll tell him to eat heartily and the same about the medicine. Then I'll ask how he is and he'll say, 'Better.' I'll say 'Praise God!' and ask him who his doctor is. He'll give me some name. I'll say that his presence is a blessing and that he's a good physician and does a good job wherever he goes. After that I'll say farewell and return home."

Thinking over this conversation, he decided that it was good and he entered the house of the sick butcher.

He greeted everyone and they replied. Then Shaban went to the side of the sick man and sat down. The butcher was very ill. Shaban put his hand on the man's arm and asked, "How are you? Are you better?"

The butcher moaned. "No way! I'm very sick. I'm dying."

"Praise God! Praise be to God!" said Shaban. "Thank God. By and by everything will be all right!"

The sick man grew more miserable. Those present were astonished at Shaban's words.

"So," Shaban continued. "What medicine are you taking? What are you eating?"

"I'm consuming the poison of death!"

"Excellent!" said the deaf man. "there is no food better than that for a sick man."

The sick butcher became even more upset! One of those present said to Shaban, "My good man, what are you saying? Are you his enemy?"

Shaban couldn't hear these words of caution. He was silent for a few moments then asked the butcher, "Who's your doctor?"

"The angel of death!" he cried weakly. "Get up and get out of here. What impudence!"

"You have a good doctor," said deaf Shaban. "He does good work wherever he goes. Whatever house he enters he finishes the job in a day."

The sick man couldn't stand it any more. "Ah! Take this fool away from me! Throw him out! What does he want from me?"

The others grabbed Shaban and kicked him out, saying, "What kind of an idiot are you? Is that the way you talk to a sick man? Do you hate him?"

"If I see that doctor," said Shaban, "I'll ask him to attend to the butcher more quickly."

One of the men pushed Shaban violently into the street and another went to beat him up when, by chance, the villager who had met Shaban at the mill that morning arrived on the scene.

"Hit him!" he cried, adding fuel to the flames. "He's not even crazy, he's just a mocker, a fool. Only a beating will straighten him out. I've already seen his tricks."

When the villager went to strike a blow, Shaban shouted, "Why are you hitting me? I didn't say anything bad! I haven't done anything!"

At this moment a young man came out of a neighboring house and saw the tumult. "Hey!," he yelled. "What's going on? Stop and let's see! Why are you beating this man up?"

"He's making fun of us. He came to a sick man and said awful things to him. And he still won't stop!"

"Let me see what's going on," said the youth. He approached Shaban and said. "Look here, man! What were you doing in that house?"

The poor deaf man thought he was being asked why he was screaming. "They want to beat me. I haven't done anything."

"You must have done something," said the young man. "What's your name?"

Shaban thought he was being asked why he had gone there. "The local butcher was sick and I came to visit him."

"Okay," said the youth. "Where do you live?"

"I don't know. It wasn't my fault."

It happened that the young man was the son of Salman the grocer and he recognized the difficulty. He thought for a moment and then said to the crowd, "Perhaps this man is deaf since he speaks all right, but his answers are wrong."

The youth pulled a pencil and paper out of a pocket and wrote, "Can you read and write?"

"Yes," said the deaf man. "I can read and write. "

The youth was certain that Shaban had not done anything wrong. "His only fault is his vanity. He doesn't want people to know that he is hard of hearing." He broke up the crowd and they went away. Then he wrote on the paper:

"Look, dear uncle, it is no sin to be deaf. My father is Salman the grocer and he is deaf. You gave inappropriate answers and upset the people. They thought you were making fun of them. If people knew that you were deaf, it would be much better for you than this humiliation. So, my dear man, say that you are deaf and save yourself a lot of trouble."

"Thanks," said Shaban. "I'm very grateful to you. You're right. I confess that once I made fun of your father for his deafness, but now I'll never make fun of anyone again. I must admit my own defect. I've made fun of myself. You are right. One must admit his failings. I am deaf."

After that day, Shaban put a piece of paper in his pocket and whenever someone asked him something, he would show him the paper. Upon it was written:

"Sir, I am deaf. I cannot hear anything. If you need to say something, please write it so that I may read it and give you an answer."

23
KAMAL AL-DIN HASAN

Once a poet had written a long poem about the New Year's Festival. In it he had included much praise for the goodness of the current king. He had worked very hard to insert as much praise as possible. On the day of the New Year's Festival he went to the royal court to read his masterpiece and collect a suitable reward and perhaps a cloak of honor.

In olden days when there were no newspapers and magazines, and there was no radio or news reports, kings and princes and ministers gave poets generous presents to put their good deeds and honors into verses that would be recited to the people. Lots of poets put all other considerations of art aside and lived on the money they received for their praise and glorification of the great. In this way both parties benefited.

Our poet had heard, too, that this particular king would give a thousand dinars for a good ode. That was why he had composed such a long one. So, after receiving permission to approach the throne, he recited his poem.

It was a beautiful poem and those present admired it very much. The king shared their opinion and whispered to a retainer, "A thousand dinars!"

He meant that the poet should be given a reward of a thousand dinars. It happened that the king had a vizier named Kamal al-Din Hasan who was a learned man, a lover of literature, and a connoisseur of poetry. Since he saw that this poet's poem was superb, he whispered to the king, "Give permission to bestow ten thousand dinars on this poet, for his poem is better than all of the others."

"Vizier!" cried the king. "What are you saying? If we spend money like that, the treasury will soon be empty! We have a thousand kinds of obligations. We can't just foster poets. There are many unresolved problems in the kingdom. There are limits for everything!"

"What you say is true, your majesty," replied Kamal al-din. "I accept that poetry in itself will not solve any problems, but everything good has its own good and is valuable. The people love poetry, and this poet, with his eloquence and taste, has a much greater value than the others. Well-chosen words are sharper than a sword. We should encourage him so that his swordlike tongue will always be employed in your service."

"That's not a bad idea," mused the king. "Very well. Do what you think best."

The vizier ordered that a purse of ten thousand dinars be given to the poet together with a suit of splendid clothing. The poet was delighted.

After receiving these presents, he said to the courtiers, "I had heard that the reward for an ode was a thousand dinars, but now I see it is much more than that. If I had known that, I would have written a far longer poem and included even better things."

"That's the way it is," was the reply. "They always give

poets a thousand dinars, but this Kamal al-Din Hasan, the king's vizier, liked your poetry so much that your reward was made ten thousand on his advice. Kamal al-Din Hasan is a learned man and a connoisseur of poetry. He wanted to show you that he recognized your merit."

"Wonderful!" said the poet. "So that's how it is!"

Then the poet went home. In order to show his appreciation and gratitude to Kamal al-Din Hasan, he wrote a longer poem praising him and sent it to the vizier's house.

With the prize money that he had received, the poet was saved from poverty and became free from worry. He was able to take care of his own affairs for a while and write poetry that he himself according to his own taste. Most of this poetry told stories and was filled with counsel and wisdom. The vizier admired this poetry, but the prince did not.

However, after some time had passed, the poet found himself in debt once more. People said to him, "You'd better write another ode and get a prize in order to straighten out your life."

So the poet sat down and wrote another lengthy poem. This one was twice as long as the first and he used every literary device he knew to embellish it. He tried to employ all the skills of his art to make it beautiful. Then he sought an audience with the king. He went to the court, took his poem out and read it.

The assembly applauded him and the king, as was his custom, called a retainer and told him to bring a thousand dinars.

But by this time the previous vizier had died and the king had a different one. This vizier had the mind of an adding machine and was very tight with money. In a low voice he said to the king, "As you majesty commands, but I imagine that a thousand dinars for a poem is rather a lot. The poet, who wrote it in one night, will be satisfied with ten dinars."

"But," said the king, "this is a very capable poet. He doesn't make it a habit of praising just anyone every day. His praise is very valuable for us. It's better that he be pleased and always commemorate our goodness."

"True," said the vizier, "but if we are to give every poet a thousand dinars who stitches together a few verses and comes here with his hand outstretched, the treasury will soon be emptied. Everyone will leave his work and his land and start writing poetry! We shouldn't encourage flattery and sycophancy."

"That's true too," said the king, "but they are the ones who spread the news about our justice and fairness throughout the land. Fair words are sharper than a sword. There is nothing wrong with this poet serving us with the sword of his tongue."

"Yes," said the vizier, "but poetry doesn't solve any problems. We have a thousand different kinds of expenses and the kingdom has a thousand unsettled problems. We should encourage the artisans. We should encourage the builders, the carpenters, the blacksmiths, and the farmers so that country will flourish. The essence of poetry is just a fistful of words. The more money the poets get, the more they lie and the more they mislead the people. If we used that money to buy candles and light the streets and lanes after dark, or to build another hall of justice, or to thwart tyranny and oppression, such works would be a hundred times better than poems."

"Yes," agreed the king, "but the poet has heard that the

reward for an ode is a thousand dinars. If we disappoint him, he may go away and criticize us."

"That's possible," replied the vizier, "but I won't disappoint him. With your permission, I shall please him with promises and assurances. By postponing and delay from one day to the next I'll keep him pleased while he waits for his money. When he's come to me a few times, he'll get tired of it. Just when he's about to give up hope, I'll give him a hundred dinars. He'll bow his head to the throne with joy and relief that he got something and didn't leave empty-handed. That is a rule of life: If you pay quickly in cash, you'll pay more and people will be less pleased. But if you pay late and less than the full amount, they'll be happy to get what you give them!"

"If that's what you say," said the king uneasily. "Anyway, I want him to depart the court pleased and satisfied."

"Your mind may rest at ease, your majesty," said the crafty vizier.

Then the vizier addressed the poet: "That was a very good poem. God bless you for it! But there is something I need to say to you. We wanted to give you a prize of one hundred thousand dinars. Yes, indeed! It's worth it! But unfortunately, we don't have more than a thousand dinars on hand today and we have many obligations. You know that better than we do. In any case, we wish to ask your excellency to give us a week to raise the money. Then I'll present you with whatever you wish!"

Hearing the sum of one hundred thousand dinars mentioned, the poet in his hunger for that said, "As you wish, your excellency. We are not ungrateful, and such material concerns are of no moment between us."

"Bravo!" exclaimed the vizier. "Now, we know and respect the value of everything. By next week I'll have thought a good present for you."

So the poet left and waited patiently for two weeks, but there was no news from the palace. On some pretext or other, he went to the vizier and said, "You yourself commanded me to come."

"Great! Welcome!" exclaimed the vizier. "Your coming delights me. I've been eager to see you again. Come in, come in! But there is one thing I must say that embarrasses me in front of you. Conditions are such that, for example, that it isn't possible to give your excellency even less than a thousand dinars! We don't have more than five hundred today, and we have many payments to make. I have you in mind. It won't take more than a month. Don't worry, everything will work out."

When the poet understood that the vizier was now talking about five hundred dinars, he got anxious. In order to not to lower the price of his goods, so to speak, he said, "As you wish, Lord Vizier. There's no need to talk about such things. But, my living standard hasn't been too good, and I have debts of more than a thousand dinars. Now circumstances have led me here. Whatever way you think is best. I'll wait until things are worked out."

"Yes, yes!" said the vizier. "I am considering ways so that you do not lose out. It will be straightened out in a month or two. I have the address of your house."

The poet went out and in that fashion summer became winter, and winter spring. Every time the vizier would say that he had a little money but it was insufficient. One time he mentioned four hundred dinars. Another time three hundred, then two hundred.

The poet could bear the promises and delays no longer. One day he got angry and went unhappily to the palace to remind the vizier still another time of his promise. He saw one of the former courtiers at the gate and recognized him. After enquiring about his health, the poet said, "I want to know the truth. How is it that last year the reward for a poem was ten thousand dinars in prompt cash and this year they talk about a thousand dinars of which there is no news or sign. I'm losing my patience."

"The problem is," said the doorkeeper, "that the former vizier has died and now the control of affairs is in the hands of another."

"Incredible!" exclaimed the poet. "God have mercy on the departed! But how is such a thing possible? I've forgotten what the previous vizier looked like, but I've seen that they call this one Kamal al-Din Hasan too."

"Yes," said the doorkeeper, "Their names are the same, but there is a great difference between them. The old one was open-hearted and generous, but this one is a dry stick! In my opinion, it would be better to take the one hundred dinars he'll give than the promise of a thousand. Take it as quickly as you can and get away from here. If not, you may have to be satisfied with the dream of even ten dinars! This vizier always promises, but we can see that there is no resemblance between this Hasan and the previous one. I wish I had figured it out sooner!"

So the poet went to the vizier and said, "I've come another time to remind you about the matter of the prize."

"Welcome! Welcome!" cried the vizier. "You've brightened my day! But there is something I must tell you. I want to give you a suitable reward, but there isn't more than the sum of a hundred dinars on hand. I'm thinking about doing something so that perhaps you can receive your just due."

"Thank you, but today something has happened that makes it better if you command that that one hundred dinars be given to me so that I may disclose to you some important news that I've learned."

The vizier thought a moment then gave him the one hundred dinars and then asked, "What was the important news! God willing, I hope it's good. How are things?"

"The important news is this," said the poet, "that until now I thought that you were Kamal al-Din Hasan. If I had known that you weren't, I would have taken the prize that was first a thousand, and then five hundred dinars. I wouldn't have waited until the matter was old and the king himself had forgotten about it, the oven grown cold, and the water passed through the mill."

"Then who do you think I am?" asked the vizier. "Am I not Kamal al-Din Hasan?"

"Certainly," answered the poet. "Your name is Kamal al-Din Hasan, but you yourself are not Kamal al-Din Hasan. I was deceived by your name. As they say, 'Whoever is deceived by a name will lose his bread.'"

24

THE GAZELLE IN THE DONKEYS' STABLE

One day a hunter caught a gazelle in the desert. At night, when he returned to his house, he saw that there was nothing to eat. However much he thought about slaughtering the gazelle to roast it, he couldn't bring himself to do that. So he took the gazelle and went to the foot of the street where there some people standing.

"This gazelle is for sale," said the hunter.

"How much?" they asked.

"It's worth fifty tomans, but as I need some money, I'll sell it for ten."

When they understood that the hunter needed money, one of the people said, "I'll buy it for two tomans."

"Three tomans," said another.

"Four tomans," said another man.

One man, a driver of beasts of burden, took a liking to the gazelle. He had a bit of money on him, so he offered five tomans. "No one is going to pay more for it at this time of night," he added. "Anyway, how much meat does a dried up, skinny gazelle have?"

"People don't buy gazelles to slaughter," said the hunter. "A gazelle is a gazelle, not a sheep!"

"So you say," the driver retorted. "Anyway, you can get five tomans from me."

So he bought the gazelle and took it home where he placed in the stable with the donkeys.

The little gazelle went in and saw that the stable was a frightening place. There were several big donkeys and several mangers. In each manger there was some hay. There was a basin of water filled with litter. The place smelled of damp and dung. The air was stifling and the door firmly shut.

While he was thinking about what he should do in this new situation, the donkeys noticed him. They looked at each other and snickered. One of the donkeys asked the small gazelle, "And who might you be?"

"I, too, am one of God's creatures," replied the gazelle. "I'm called a gazelle. I was living in the desert when someone caught me and brought me home. Then he sold me to your master. Then he placed me here."

"Very good," said the donkeys. "Whoever you are, welcome! This is a very good place. Look, the basin is full of water and the mangers full of hay. No one comes here to bother us until morning. You are our guest! Come, eat your fill and take your rest wherever you want, but be careful not get trampled on."

"Many thanks, now that I am here," said the gazelle. "But I can't drink that water or eat that hay. You keep on doing what you were doing. I'll be in one of the corners."

So the donkeys applied themselves to the food and went from one manger to another. They jostled each other and ran about the stable raising dust and dirt. The gazelle fled from one corner to another to keep out of their way and from fear of being trampled upon. He was overcome with fright, misery, the dusty air, and the stable's smell.

From time to time the donkeys looked at the gazelle and gestured to each other. They laughed at him and said, "Look at the gazelle! What a strange animal! His legs are as thin as the tube of a water pipe. Look at his horns! Look at his eyes! He doesn't resemble anything alive! And he doesn't eat anything and doesn't speak. He runs from one corner to another and is afraid of us. He thinks we're boogeymen!"

And they all laughed again.

One of the gentler donkeys said, "Look, he's not like us and he's a stranger here. Perhaps he's afraid of us because he's a small infant. Whatever he is, he's our guest and he should be made comfortable. We shouldn't do anything to frighten him more."

They all admitted that he was right and calmed down.

Then the gentle donkey said to the gazelle, "Come, dear child. Come here beside me. Eat in my manger. See how good the hay is? Yellow like saffron, thick like the leaves of the trees, soft like moist alfalfa. Sweet like a melon rind. Don't be afraid! No one will bother you. Come and have your dinner."

"I'm very grateful for your kindness," said the gazelle, "but I'm not a child. My race is small and delicate. My body is small, but for my part, I'm mature and fully grown. If I were a man and not a gazelle, you would consider me an old man."

The donkeys all laughed at such an absurd statement. One of them said, "So you're not a child, but an old man.

Come here, old man. Come beside me and eat some barley."

The donkeys laughed again.

"I don't want anything," said the gazelle. "Hay and barley are good for you, because you're used to such food. My teeth can't chew hay and barley. Please, just leave me alone."

"Aha!" exclaimed one of the donkeys. "I understand. This old man doesn't have any teeth. Poor old man! Tell us, what did you eat in the desert? Did you eat the wind? Did someone cook noodle stew for you?"

All of the donkeys laughed.

"Please don't make fun of me," cried the gazelle. "Alas! You don't understand. I'm suffocating here. A stable full of donkeys is not a place for me. I don't want to insult you, but a donkey is a donkey and a gazelle is a gazelle. Each has been created differently. I used to roam grassy places in the desert and eat fresh alfalfa. You see that I am not at fault."

"Okay, okay!" said one of the donkeys impatiently. "Now that we have encouraged him, just see how grandly he talks! He's suffocating here! Green meadows and fresh alfalfa! A gazelle isn't a donkey! The wretch doesn't like hay and barley as good as ours and wants us to give him fresh alfalfa! You're the donkey! Forget him and let him die from hunger."

"That is what I want," said the gazelle. "Leave me alone and don't make fun of me."

The gazelle had become very sad and didn't know what to do. His eyes filled with tears and he thought to himself, "I wish that the hunter had thrown me in a well and not caused me to come here. Any fate is better for me than living with these malicious dolts."

When the donkey who was the gentlest of the lot saw the tears of the gazelle, he felt sorry for him and went to him. "Look, dear friend, don't cry. It doesn't do any good. Remember the old saying: 'laugh at the world so that the world may smile at you.'

"Look at us. We laugh and we don't weep. We feel as sad about our lives as you do, but what can we do? Now that your fate has brought you to this stable, you too be like us. Talk, listen, laugh, and don't worry so much! If you say the stable is bad, so it's bad! Get used to it the way we have done. We would be much happier in a garden and would like to graze on fresh alfalfa, but when we can't, we can't! Don't kill yourself!

"Believe me, hay is also tasty. If you eat hay and barley as we do, you'll get bigger and become a distinguished animal. But if you want the fresh alfalfa, I'll pick out all of it that is in our food and give it to you."

But when the gazelle saw that they didn't understand what he had been saying, he choked with anger and couldn't answer.

At that moment, one of the donkeys cried from a corner of the stable, "Look here! I've found a piece of fresh alfalfa! Friends, put every piece of fresh alfalfa that you find aside for the gazelle. If you want to do a good deed, give it all to the gazelle. His weeping has filled my heart with pity. Let's not let him cry. God wouldn't like it!"

"You don't have to feel sorry for me," said the gazelle. "Even your pity is stupid and foolish. I'm not a beggar to be given alms on the roadside for the pleasure of God! You're the beggars! You can't understand me because you're donkeys and I'm a gazelle!"

The donkeys turned away and said, "What is this? What a strange, stupid animal you are! We are treating you well and you aim sarcastic remarks at us?"

One of them said, "The devil is telling me to give him a kick in the head!"

Another said, "He wants fresh alfalfa, but he won't accept any favors from us!"

A third said, "I'll teach him a lesson!"

And he went to the gazelle and kicked him in the leg. Another bit his shoulder. The gazelle fainted from fright and pain.

But the gentle donkey said, "You've done wrong. It's not his fault. There are thousands of kinds of animals in the world; he is one of them. There are many kinds that think and live differently from us. We eat hay and barley. A gazelle doesn't. That isn't a sin and there's no need to beat him up. You've done a very bad thing in attacking him."

"It's really your fault," said the other donkeys. "You started to spoil him from the very beginning. You made him cry. If you hadn't, his hunger would have forced him to eat this hay and exclaim 'delicious!'"

Morning dawned and the animal driver came to the stable to take the donkeys out to work. He saw the gazelle fallen to one side gasping for breath. He picked it up and put it on his shoulders. Then he carried it to the house of the hunter.

"Look, brother, I don't have any place to keep it except the stable. I put him there last night. It's obvious that the donkeys don't get along with the gazelle. They kicked it and now I feel sorry for it. Take it back and decide what to do with it. Whenever you get some money, give me my five tomans back."

So the hunter took the gazelle back and cared for it until it got better. Then he took it to a zoo and sold it for fifty tomans out of which he repaid the animal driver.

The gazelle was put in the gazelle cage. Since he was very happy he laughed, but the other gazelles taunted him, saying, "What a strange, carefree gazelle you are! It's a good thing that you can be so happy in this prison. Where did you come from?"

"From hell," he replied. "I'm happy because, whatever it is, we speak the same language. I've seen much worse than this. In comparison with the donkeys' stable, this place is paradise. Life with the hateful and unworthy is worse than hell!"